WITHDRAWN FROM
COLLECTION

RENEGADE RANGER

Center Point
Large Print

Books are produced in the United States using U.S.-based materials

Books are printed using a revolutionary new process called THINKtech™ that lowers energy usage by 70% and increases overall quality

Books are durable and flexible because of smythe-sewing

Paper is sourced using environmentally responsible foresting methods and the paper is acid-free

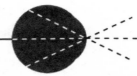

This Large Print Book carries the Seal of Approval of N.A.V.H.

RENEGADE RANGER

Jim Kane

CENTER POINT LARGE PRINT
THORNDIKE, MAINE

This Center Point Large Print edition is published in the year 2017 by arrangement with Golden West Literary Agency.

First US edition: Arcadia House. First UK edition: Muller.

The text of this Large Print edition is unabridged. In other aspects, this book may vary from the original edition. Printed in the United States of America on permanent paper. Set in 16-point Times New Roman type.

ISBN: 978-1-68324-453-0 (hardcover) ISBN: 978-1-68324-457-8 (paperback)

Library of Congress Cataloging-in-Publication Data

Names: Kane, Jim, 1913–1983, author.
Title: Renegade ranger / Jim Kane.
Description: Center Point Large Print edition. | Thorndike, Maine : Center Point Large Print, 2017.
Identifiers: LCCN 2017014427| ISBN 9781683244530 (hardcover : alk. paper) | ISBN 9781683244578 (pbk. : alk. paper)
Subjects: LCSH: Large type books. | GSAFD: Western stories.
Classification: LCC PS3505.O6646 R465 2017 | DDC 813/.54—dc23
LC record available at https://lccn.loc.gov/2017014427

RENEGADE RANGER

Luke Riatt had grown up in a world which the War Between the States had ended forever. He had been eighteen when Lee had surrendered; and defeat had left a bitter taste in his mouth. His marriage had ended abruptly when cholera had killed his wife and child. Since then he had drifted, a lonely man with lonely assignments. But now, after fifteen years of solitude, he was teaming up with another Ranger to ride into Crown Basin and to keep the peace along the Texas-Mexico border.

The difficulty was that Luke's fellow Ranger was one of the "wild Stringer clan" and that some of his own family were working with a renegade gang which wanted to rid the country of the law. Which left Luke with quite a weak reed to lean on.

CHAPTER ONE

The cracked shades were drawn tight against the Border sun, and a breath of morning coolness lingered inside Del Rio's adobe jail.

Luke Riatt shifted his heavy .45-70 rifle to his left hand and signaled to Felipe Mendoza, who stood waiting by the back door. The *jefe* unlocked it and squinted out into the alley. He had a gun in his hand, but his survey was merely precautionary; he wasn't expecting any trouble.

He turned and nodded perfunctorily to Luke.

Riatt put a hand on his prisoner's shoulder and shoved him toward the door. The man, his hands cuffed in front of him, took three forced steps forward, then balked. Crossing his legs, he sat down, his face sullen and rebellious.

Luke walked to him and looked down. The heat that came in from the alley was an unpleasant foretaste of the ride ahead of him; it did little to improve his disposition.

"You can get up and walk through that door and get on that horse, Malino," he said flatly, "or I can carry you out and dump you across the saddle!"

Malino eyed him with bright wickedness. He

was a wiry breed, part Yaqui, three quarters white, and in him these elements had fused into a mean combination. He waited, judging the temper of this big man standing over him. Then, as Riatt shifted his grip on the rifle, he came to his feet, his mouth turning down in bitter defeat.

Riatt pushed him through the doorway into the alley, where two horses waited slack-hipped in the still heavy heat of Del Rio's siesta hour.

Felipe Mendoza waited in the doorway, concern causing his jowly, dark-bearded face to twitch. He knew Riatt from before, and understood the stamp of loneliness on this big, raw-boned man. But there was an uneasiness in Felipe as he watched, and it was not entirely inspired by the prisoner.

Riatt boosted the recalcitrant Malino into the saddle of the runty gray horse he had hired at the local livery stable and further secured him by tying Malino's legs under the belly of the animal.

Sliding his rifle into the saddle boot, he mounted the thick-chested roan, then turned his attention to Del Rio's *jefe.* His voice was kindly.

"Better get some rest, man. You look beat."

Felipe made a tired gesture. "I'll sleep after you have gone."

Riatt lingered a moment, studying the stocky Mexican lawman. He felt a little sorry for Felipe. Malino was a first cousin of the Cordero

10

brothers, and they would look with little favor on anyone who had helped Riatt.

"I couldn't make Chuckawalla Wells last night," he said quietly. "You know that, Felipe? I had to put him up here."

Felipe shrugged. "It is a worry," he admitted. "But I was thinking of your partner, Luke."

"Lee?"

Felipe nodded. "He is waiting for you?"

"Across the plaza, at Sam Stark's store." Tightness edged Luke's mouth. "He's checking the mail."

"Ah," Felipe murmured, "I had forgotten. He always checks the mail when he comes to Del Rio."

"A man has friends," Luke replied coldly.

"And relatives," Felipe added harshly. "Like old Buck Stringer!"

"Like Buck Stringer," Riatt repeated. "He didn't try to hide it, Felipe."

"Then perhaps he has changed, Luke." But the *jefe*'s tone held disbelief. "They say even the wild ones change, when they become Rangers."

"You knew Lee Stringer?"

"I jailed him . . . last year. It was the time of the fiesta of Santa Margerita . . . he was disturbing the peace." Felipe paused, remembering . . . His tone, when he spoke again, held an odd warning.

"I will be glad when he, too, is gone from Del Rio, Luke."

11

Luke settled back in the saddle. "You worry too much, Felipe," he said shortly.

"Perhaps." Felipe smiled tiredly. "One gets old . . ." He raised his hand in farewell. "Be careful of him, Luke . . ."

The alley from which Luke emerged led into Del Rio's small, dusty plaza, and the ugly brown hills rose almost directly behind the town, hot and repellingly arid at that time of day.

Luke let his horse turn to the adobe trough under the gnarled pepper tree in the center of the plaza. The shade felt good against his face. Malino sat unmoving, his sullenness like a *serape* wrapped around him.

Sam Stark's store was directly ahead . . . a long adobe structure with a deep covered veranda. Sam was one of the few gringos in Del Rio. . . . He had settled there early, marrying a Mexican wife and thriving on the border trade. Once a week the regular stage to Nueva Cuidad detoured to drop off mail and an occasional passenger. . . . Otherwise Del Rio's contact with the rest of the world was meager, a condition entirely acceptable to the town's two hundred and fifty inhabitants.

Lee Stringer's big dun nosed the rack in front of the store, and while he waited for his partner to come out, Riatt let his thoughts run past the squalid buildings to the desolate and ragged hills beyond.

He was a big man, honed down to bone and gristle and the long hard muscles of a man trained to move fast and smoothly. Sitting there in the noonday heat, he could remember leaner and more unpleasant times. He had been a green replacement with General Sibley's retreating Confederate forces in 1865 as they had straggled back that way into West Texas. . . . The harsh contours of that dry and forbidding country had been ground into him—every wash and gully and naked spur of rock.

He had been eighteen then, and the taste of defeat had burned sour in his mouth . . . and the fifteen years since Lee's surrender had not laid gentle hands on him.

His father had died and his mother had gone to live with a married sister and the world he had known before the War had disappeared. He had taken any job to keep alive, drifting out of Texas because he hated what it had become.

He married in Wyoming and took root, but he knew the responsibility of husband and father for only two short years. Then cholera had taken his woman and child and left him alone again, to drift over the savage land like a lonely Apache.

He had returned to Texas and, after a year as a civilian scout for the Army, had joined the Texas Rangers. The Army had been the only home he had known away from home, and it seemed natural, eventually, to come back to an organization that provided him with a purpose and a sense of belonging.

But Luke remained essentially a lonely man and he was given lonely assignments. This was one of the few times he had worked with a partner.

Captain John D. Hughes, commanding Company D, of which Riatt was a member, was charged with keeping the peace along a stretch of Texas-Mexican border where the law, in 1880, was a fluid and sometime thing. The Cordero brothers, Matilde and Ramon, with guts and brains had pulled together a loose organization from the scum and malcontents from both sides of the Border . . . and were raiding Mexico and Texas indiscriminately.

The Corderos were hard to trap; they slipped easily across the Border into Chihuahua and back again. They had a hideout in the hills just south of the Texas line, and Captain Hughes, stung by impatience, wanted to know where. This had been Luke's assignment; and he had assigned Lee Stringer to Riatt, on the excuse that Lee, having grown up in that part of Texas, would be of help.

But Riatt had sensed there was more behind the Captain's order than this, and had faced him with it.

Hughs had been frank. "All right, Luke . . . so he is a wild kid! Old Buck Stringer's boy! But

14

what he needs right now is a friend . . . someone who can get close to him. He's on the edge, Luke—he can go either way, bad or good. Give him a hand."

"I'm not the man he needs," Riatt had said, and tried to back out of it. But Hughes had teamed them together anyway; and waiting here now, Luke knew it had been as much his fault as Lee's that it had not worked out.

Lee Stringer was a hard man to know. He was seven years younger than Luke, and he rode with a deep-seated discontent which he had shown little inclination to discuss.

They had run Malino and his partner down after they had shot and robbed a storekeeper. . . . Malino's partner had died with a bullet through his head. They were taking Malino to Chuckawalla Wells to catch the through stage to El Paso . . . and Luke had made up his mind to tell Captain Hughes when they arrived he was through riding with Lee.

A door creaked in the stillness, and he pulled his thoughts back. Lee came out of Stark's store, a tall, muscular, straw-haired man with a narrow, sensitive face and brooding gray eyes. He walked slowly to the head of the stairs and stopped, his gaze moving down the street, apparently not seeing Riatt or not wanting to.

He stood and read his letter again; then he crumpled it in his fist, and something in his tight face shocked Riatt. He pulled his horse away from the trough and rode to the store.

"Bad news, kid?"

Stringer didn't answer him. The knuckles, tightened over the letter he had been reading, showed white against the deep brown of his skin.

Luke dismounted, walked up to him and put a hand on Lee's shoulder. "If there's anything I can do—?"

Lee jerked away. "You can't!" he snapped. "And keep yore blasted hands off me!"

Luke checked the upsurge of his temper, but it left a bitter taste in his mouth. "Sure. Forget I asked."

Lee's mouth was pinched, as though he were hurt deep inside. But he forced a faint gesture of apology. "Letter from home, Luke. No concern of yours."

Luke nodded. "All right. We better get riding."

"You go ahead," Lee said. "I'll join you."

"The stage runs on a tight schedule," Luke reminded him. "It won't wait."

"I said I'd be there!"

Behind Luke Malino stirred, a glitter of expectancy appearing in his black eyes. Luke sensed this and forced the anger out of his tone.

"Need something?"

"A drink!" Lee looked at Riatt, flat defiance in his eyes. There was something wild and ugly in him at that moment that puzzled Luke.

He nodded. "I'll have one with you—at the bar across the plaza!"

"Right friendly of you!" Lee sneered. He thrust his crumpled letter into his pants pocket and slowly wiped his sweaty palm on his trousers. "Big Luke Riatt finally breaks down and invites himself to drink with Buck Stringer's son!" He sucked in a harsh breath. "Well, the devil with you! I ain't drinking with—"

Luke's left hand shot out, the fingers hooking into Lee's shirt. . . . His right hand clamped down hard on Lee's right wrist, forestalling the younger man's instinctive motion toward his Colt.

"You'll have your drink," Luke breathed coldly, "without me! But you're riding to Chuckawalla Wells with me, and we're taking Malino into El Paso together!" He paused a moment, then added wickedly: "After that I don't give a hoot in Hades what you do, kid!"

He shoved Lee away from him.

The youngster's tanned face was white . . . boyhood freckles showed up now, like liver spots on the back of an old man's hand.

"Sure," he acquiesced. "I'll ride to Chuckawalla Wells with you. But I won't be going on to El Paso. . . ."

CHAPTER TWO

Chuckawalla Wells lay to the north at the end of a long dry ride eleven miles from Del Rio.

Tim Culver, station agent, met them in the yard, shielding his eyes against the glare of the afternoon sun. Culver was an old, stringy man with a thatch of white hair and an easy disposition.

He looked at the identification and badge Riatt used to identify himself, glanced at Lee, then at Malino. His eyes grew troubled.

"Didn't know you had a prisoner. It might complicate things."

Riatt frowned. "How?"

"Just got word this morning. Regular shotgun guard took sick at Red Bluffs. The stage's coming through here with only the driver, Ben Nesbitt." He glanced worriedly at Malino again. "Bad time to have trouble, mister."

"Why?"

"There's twenty thousand in gold riding on that stage. And there's men out here who'd kill for a fraction of that!"

"We'll ride guard on it as far as El Paso," Luke answered shortly. He dismounted, gestured to Malino. "Got a place where we can keep him until the stage arrives?"

Culver shook his head. "No need, anyway. Stage's due in a half-hour—"

Lee cut in, his voice tight, almost flat. "Any passengers?"

"Two. Man and wife, I hear."

Riatt turned to Lee, but the younger man was staring off into the distance, toward the low sand hills flanking the stage road.

Culver said: "Come inside. I got beer on ice in back. You boys care for a drink?"

Luke nodded. "Sounds fine. . . ."

He untied Malino and pulled him out of saddle. Lee dismounted slowly; he was strangely quiet, subdued.

Riatt ignored him. He figured Lee was sulking over whatever bad news he seemed to have received, and also the tongue lashing he had taken from Luke. But the disquiet persisted in Riatt; a small, nagging thing he could not shake off.

They followed the station attendant inside. Riatt motioned Malino to a chair with his rifle. . . . Malino walked to it and sat down slowly, as though on eggs. He was tense, alert, like a trapped animal waiting for the slightest break. . . .

Culver went on toward the back of the building. . . . His voice lifted through the

19

comparative coolness of the adobe station: ". . . Heard Captain Hughs might be relieved of his command. . . ."

He returned with three bottles, uncapped, and three glasses. . . . He glanced at Malino.

"What about him?"

"He'll drink water . . . later," Riatt replied coldly. Culver shrugged and sat down. "One of the Cordero gang?"

Riatt nodded. "He killed a storekeeper in Ysleta. We're taking him in to El Paso."

Culver looked worried. "There's rumors the Cordero bunch is getting guns . . . new Army Winchesters."

Riatt sipped his beer. He was not a talkative man, and on this subject he was close-mouthed. He knew how the settlements along the sparsely populated border felt about the Corderos. They were growing to be a worry, and they worried the Mexican Rurales, too. But the Mexican troops took the reasonable view that as long as they confined their depradations to the American side, they, in turn, would make no concerted attempt to run them down.

To the poor peons across the Line, the Corderos were beginning to assume the proportions of a Robin Hood. A peon subsisting on a goat or two and a half-acre of beans would often find a butchered beef on his doorstep, or a few gold coins in a jar on his window sill.

In return he kept his mouth closed about the Corderos, hid them out when they needed it. It was a simple arrangement, and understandable. But it did not lessen the threat to the settlements across the Border, and there were some now who were growing impatient with Company D's strict observance of the international boundary.

Riatt understood Culver's concern. . . . He knew what fifty or a hundred new repeating rifles in the hands of Cordero's ragged *bandidos* could mean. . . . Something like that same concern, he thought, must be felt by the Governor of Chihuahua, for power was a two-edged sword along the Texas Border.

Culver got up and went back for three more bottles; he returned and was just settling his wiry frame on the bench when a dog began to bark excitedly in the back yard.

"That'll be the stage," he said, getting up. He was relieved of the necessity of making small talk. "Tanker always lets me know when it tops the hill yonder."

He turned and headed for the door. Stringer came to his feet, a bright and bitter look in his eyes that caught Riatt's attention.

Luke said, "Finish your beer, Lee. We've got plenty of time."

Lee ignored him and headed after Culver.

The sense of disquiet gripped Riatt hard now. Malino was watching him, eyes bright, as if he sensed something in the wind. Riatt hesitated, then jerked a thumb toward the front door.

Malino held back. He mumbled, "Water," and licked dry lips expectantly.

Riatt turned to look after Lee. The younger Ranger was already going through the open door, out into the glaring sunlight of the yard. Riatt shifted his rifle to his left, reached over and jerked Malino to his feet. "You'll get your water later!" he snapped.

He didn't understand his own urgency, but something pulled him toward the yard.

He shoved the balky Malino ahead of him, his stride long and hurried. . . .

The stage wheeled into the station, its iron tires raising a cloud of white alkali dust which drifted slowly toward the corrals. The driver brought it around in a sharp half-circle and pulled up by the door, the coach rocking on its leather springs. . . . The driver looked down at Culver waiting, loosed a stream of tobacco juice over the rump of the left wheeler and calmly began wrapping the reins around the whip handle.

Culver walked to the stage, grinned at the leathery, blue-eyed man on the seat and said: "Got a gun escort for you, Ben." He waved to Stringer coming through the doorway. "Couple of Rangers taking a prisoner into El Paso."

Ben managed to grin through the alkali

powdering his rough features. "Shore glad to have 'em. That box in my boot doesn't ride easy."

Culver reached for the door handle, opened it and stepped back as a tall, well-dressed man with full sideburns and a gambling man's cool appraisal emerged. The man turned immediately to help a smiling, full-bosomed woman down the iron step.

"Twenty minutes rest, ma'am," Culver informed her.

The woman paused on the iron step to stare with indifferent interest at Culver, at the dingy way station. Then her attention went to Stringer by the door. He moved toward them as she looked, and the smile froze on her face and her features stiffened as though an icy wind had come out of nowhere to freeze them.

Her hand tightened convulsively on the shoulder of her companion. She said: *"Lee!"* in a shocked, strangled voice.

The tall man with her whirled quickly. He saw Stringer's striding figure and his right hand darted inside his coat. . . . The woman cried, *"Lee!"* again just as a gun appeared in Stringer's hand and blasted heavily in the stillness.

Stringer emptied his gun at the man. The passenger jerked and twisted to the smash of lead—he fell against the woman, and the lead kept smashing into him.

The woman stared down at her husband as he

slid limply against the wheel. Up on the seat Ben had grabbed the reins and with a firm hand was keeping the horses from bolting.

For a few seconds the woman looked down on the dead man, her face deathly white. Blood began making a dark stain against the brown taffeta of her traveling coat.

"Lee," she whispered, "you shouldn't—" She licked her lips with the point of her tongue; then her legs caved under her. She fell in an odd-shaped heap across the body of the man listed on the passenger manifest as her husband.

Malino had halted in the doorway at the first sound of gunfire . . . he twisted now, trying to get back inside. Riatt caught only a glimpse of what went on, and he was uncertain of who had drawn on whom. He shoved Malino roughly out of his way and came out.

Stringer whirled on him: "Don't try anything, Luke—don't even make a move!"

He was drawn tight as a drum, his eyes glazed, and Riatt should have sensed this. But he didn't believe Stringer would shoot, and so he took a step toward the man, lifting his rifle up before him.

Malino slammed into him from behind, using head and shoulders as a battering ram. The impact sent Riatt staggering; and Stringer clubbed Luke across the head, a hard, glancing blow that sent the big Ranger sprawling.

Malino made a dive for the rifle Luke dropped. Stringer brought his knee up into Malino's face, driving his head backward. Blood spurted from Malino's nose.

Lee pulled the rifle from Malino's weakened grasp, clubbed him across the head, then whirled and fired as Ben, pulling his rifle from its boot, snapped a shot at him.

The driver jerked and fell sidewise, groaning; his rifle slid to the ground. He lay across the seat, gritting his teeth against the pain.

Lee motioned to Culver with the rifle. "Get up there and toss down the strongbox!"

Culver obeyed. He watched silently as the lean Ranger shot the lock off the Wells Fargo box, then stuffed money into his saddle bags.

Stringer turned to stand over the body of the woman. . . . His skin was tight across his dark cheeks and his eyes burned with a deep, dark hurt. He took five twenties from his pocket and tossed them at Culver's feet.

"See that *she* gets a decent burial," he said. His voice was as thin as rim ice. Turning, he touched the gambler's body with his toe. "You can dump *him*," he added callously, "into any desert hole!"

He walked back to his cayuse, tossed Riatt's rifle over the corral fence, then mounted. From the saddle he looked down at Luke's sprawled figure.

"I didn't want it this way," he said slowly. "You

can tell him that for me." His voice tightened bitterly. "He'll know where to find me . . . if he wants to!"

He wheeled his horse, flat-spurred it into a dead run out of the station yard.

Culver broke into a run for the rifle he kept in the station, then stopped. It was a useless gesture. He turned and walked back to the stage and climbed up to the seat where Ben was trying to sit up.

"Ranger, eh?" Ben gritted. "A lobo, that's what he was! Killed both of them in cold blood, and then robbed the stage!"

Culver turned and looked at Luke. His voice held a harsh accusation. "They were partners. Reckon that big feller'll have some explaining to do, Ben. . . ."

CHAPTER THREE

The stage left Chuckawalla Wells three hours late. A grim-faced Luke, nursing an aching head and a bitter impatience, drove.

Ben Nesbitt lay across one of the padded seats inside, his shoulder swathed in an emergency bandage. Malino sat on the roof, his right hand cuffed to the baggage railing. He crouched and watched Luke's back, his eyes smoldering with hate.

Luke drove as far as Ysleta, arriving at midnight. The stage had an overnight stay here, and he took the time to wire Captain Hughes what had happened. He received a prompt reply in the morning.

"Get Stringer. Bring him back to stand trial."

Riatt turned Malino over to the local law, ate a late breakfast, and rode back to Chuckawalla Wells.

The woman and the man Lee had killed had been interred. Culver had followed instructions and buried both of them on the hill behind the station.

Luke checked the manifest. The passengers were listed as Mr. and Mrs. John Mason— destination, El Paso.

Culver laid their personal belongings out on the counter inside the station. "The woman knew him, Luke. She called him Lee. . . ." He shrugged. "She must have known him pretty well."

Riatt nodded. He was examining the two letters Culver had found in the dead man's coat. The contents included little of interest, but the envelopes told him that they had been mailed in New Orleans and addressed to "Slick Mason, care of Shawlee's Store, Glass Mountains, Texas."

Culver looked at Riatt. "That's Buck Stringer's country . . . Crown Basin."

Riatt offered no comment. As he tucked the letters back inside their envelopes, Culver asked: "You riding that way?"

Luke nodded.

Culver indicated the personal baggage. "These things will be right here if anyone wants to claim them. Unless you want to impound them?"

"Keep them," Riatt answered. He walked outside and stood a moment, staring toward the hills, remembering that taut wildness in Lee Stringer as he had whirled to face him. It had been the look of a deeply hurt man.

Lee had killed a man and a woman, and whatever reasons he may have had for doing so, he still had to account to the law.

Those were his orders, and Luke intended to carry them out.

• • •

Broken Crown was a towering wall of limestone rimming Crown Basin. It made a crescent, with one end anchored to the grim and desolate Glass Mountains, the other petering out in the arid deserts of Chihuahua.

For more than fifty miles only two breaks in the wall gave access to the little known country behind it. One was at North Pass, rising steeply above Tortilla Flats. The other was in Mexico.

Shawlee's Store lay close to the base of the wall, clinging like some stubborn wart to the side of North Pass. It was close to sundown, and the air pressing down on the adobe building was furnace hot, the forerunner of a day of scorching sunshine. In the area behind the building the iron vanes of the wind pump hung still. . . . Below it two saddled horses bearing the Broken Crown brand hugged the shade of an old pepper tree.

Up front and close to the corral which faced the wagon road, in plain view of anyone coming through North Pass, a trim bay gelding hitched to a buggy tugged impatiently at reins looped over the top bar of the enclosure. The gelding had been tied up there since morning and it was thirsty.

Inside, in the comparative coolness of the building, Peter Shawlee leaned on his elbows and stared stonily across the short, plank bar top at the two men and the girl sitting around the table by the far wall. He kept telling himself it was none of his business what the Stringers did, but anger kept rising up in his throat like heartburn.

The girl sat very quietly, looking down at the table top. There was a beer in front of her, but it had long since gone flat. She had not touched it. On her face was a livid bruise where Vince Stringer, the tall, balding, leathery-faced man sitting next to her, had slapped her.

Shawlee didn't like to see a girl mistreated. But she was Stringer's niece, and he kept telling himself it was none of his business what the Stringers did. . . .

Ed Beadle, the shorter, bull-necked rider for the Stringer Broken Crown outfit, finished his fourth beer and wiped his mouth with the back of his hand. He was a muscular, arrogant man in his late twenties who could handle a gun well enough to work for Broken Crown. He needed a shave. He was not a patient man, and it had been all of three hours since they had walked in on the girl. Now he stirred, pushed his empty glass aside and got to his feet. He walked to the door and squinted across the rising slant of sun-beaten ground toward the cliff where North Pass made an irregular crack in the limestone wall.

He turned to Vince. "No sign yet. Mebbe he got cold feet. Mebbe he was just giving her a time—"

"He'll come!" Vince Stringer snapped. "He's

just young enough, and fool enough, to think he can get away with it!"

Beadle directed his heavy gaze on the girl. She was young and slim and she looked Mexican—she was eighteen and as much a woman as she would ever be. And Beadle, eyeing her with a sudden eagerness, figured that some day Buck would have to let her go.

The flash of reflected sunlight hit the side of the door and he turned quickly, squinting up at the rim of the limestone wall. It was close to a thousand yards to the point directly above the Pass; he couldn't make out the man behind the signaling hand mirror. But he guessed it was Slim Meeker.

He turned quickly to the man inside. "He's coming through, Vince!"

The girl's body stiffened; a tremor went through her. Vince put a hard hand on her shoulder, his fingers digging into the soft flesh with cruel warning. "Don't make a sound! Don't even move!"

He turned and spoke sharply to Beadle. "Get back in here! If he spots you he'll spook!"

Beadle walked back to the table. He didn't sit down. He leaned back against the wall behind the girl and rested his calloused palm on the walnut handle of his Colt.

Across the room Shawlee cut in bluntly: "Take yore fightin' away from here, Vince!" He was a tall, spare-framed man with a thatch of white hair over a narrow, Indian-dark face. He was part Crow, and there was an air of aloofness about him as he made a detached and calculated appraisal of the situation.

Vince eyed him impatiently. "Just tend to your own business," he suggested. "This ain't none of your affair, Peter."

Shawlee's mouth tightened. He had a wife and three children in the back room; he didn't want any trouble with Broken Crown.

Vince turned around to face the girl. "You'll learn the hard way, Rosalie. Nobody leaves Crown Basin without your father's say-so, not even his daughter!"

The girl had kept her eyes down on the table, her manner resigned and submissive. But she raised her face now, and defiance flared in the depth of her dark eyes.

"The only man who ever treated me nice," she whispered. "You can't kill him for that!"

"Treated you nice, all right," Beadle sneered from behind her. "Only man who ever got to—"

"Shut up!" Vince cut him off.

Beadle's thick lips pouted with sullen anger, but he kept a rein on his temper. Sixty-year-old Vince was still no slouch with that southpaw draw of his.

"Treated you so well you decided to run off with him," Vince continued to the girl. "You're just like that tramp sister-in-law of yours!" He laughed harshly. "An' you know what happened to her!"

"It wasn't her fault," Rosalie Stringer answered with weakening defiance. "She'd never have run off with that gambling man if—"

Her voice was muffled abruptly as Vince suddenly clasped a hand over her mouth. He stood up, dragging her to her feet with him.

He looked at Beadle. "Reckon he's come, Ed. We'll wait until he pulls up to the hitchrack; then we'll step out an' say hello."

CHAPTER FOUR

Luke Riatt eyed North Pass from the vantage point of a turn in the road. He had pulled aside to give the big roan under him a blow, for he had been pushing the animal hard since he had left Ysleta.

Now he sat slack in saddle, feeling the heat of the sun against his back. Behind that towering wall was a little known country where Buck Stringer ruled. . . . Once he rode through that dark cut the badge pinned to the inside of his coat would become meaningless.

Yet he knew what he had to do. Lee Stringer had turned renegade, and he had to be brought to justice, or Ranger law would be suspect along the entire Texas Border.

He was on high ground, two thousand feet above Tortilla Flats baking in the sun below him. Turning, he could see the far run of land fading to the lead-colored horizon. The town of Rincon, seven miles away, squalid and inconsequential, was hidden behind a tawny fold of earth.

Though the Stringers bossed Broken Crown, their iron influence reached as far as Rincon, and men there had been close-mouthed in response to

Luke's questions. A hard-bitten teamster had finally answered Luke, measuring the tall Ranger with a bold stare.

"Yup—you'll find the old ruts of a wagon track south of here. Foller them an' they'll lead yuh to North Pass."

So he had come this way, and a mile ahead, small and lost under the towering wall, was Shawlee's Store, where the man Lee Stringer had killed had once received his mail.

Riatt shifted in the saddle, his gaze studying the lonely outpost, and he had the suddenly disquieting feeling that if trouble came, it would come to him from that store.

Up on the rim of Broken Crown, Meeker, a slim, cold-eyed man, slid into his pocket the pocket mirror with which he had signalled to Vince below and raised a pair of field glasses to his eyes. He had watched Riatt come riding up the road from Rincon. . . . Now he turned to the big, hump-shouldered man crouched just back from the rim and motioned to him. The big man came up, crawling on his stomach, took the glasses away from Meeker and studied the rider on the roan.

"Vince and Ed can handle Coley Prindle," Meeker muttered. "But what about him!"

Mel Stringer scowled. Oldest of the Stringer boys, he had a craggy, swarthy face that looked as though it had been stepped on while it was still plastic. There was a coarse brutality in his yellowish eyes and thick, sensual lips, and a cruel anticipation twitched his mouth as he studied the rider below.

"Lee said he'd come," he growled.

"Who is he?"

Mel acted as though he hadn't heard the question. "Long shot for that Winchester of yore's, Slim." He slid his heavy bore rifle up alongside his cheek and checked the sighting. He spat over the side of the cliff.

"We'll see what I can do with my ol' buff'ler gun!"

Flies buzzed drowsily before the open door of Shawlee's Store as Luke Riatt rode up to the sagging hitchrack. The Broken Crown horses were tied up behind the building and therefore out of his line of vision, but he put his glance on the buggy drawn up by the pepper tree, noticing the portmanteau bag in back of the seat.

Shawlee's looked like a lonely, out-of-the-way place, and Luke wondered briefly what was the reason for its existence. Few travelers came that way, for there was nothing beyond Broken Crown except the far reaches of Chihuahua desert.

But some vague warning nagged at him. Despite the shabby innocence of the place, he had a sudden sense of uneasiness. The buggy seemed harmless enough, and so was the shaggy

36

dog which came nosing around the corner of the building.

His spine tingled slightly as some vague impulse alerted him; he turned to look up to the rim of the towering limestone wall. The sun was in his face and he could see nothing, and he silently cursed his attack of nerves.

He was about to dismount when Vince Stringer stepped out to the ramshackle stoop. He appeared abruptly, pulling the girl with him, shoving her around and in front of him. His hand was on his gun butt when he brought up short, a surprised grunt spilling from him.

Ed Beadle filled the doorway behind Vince. He had a gun in his hand, but he lowered it as he looked at Riatt. He shot a glance up to the limestone rim, wondering if Meeker's signal had been not to warn them about Coley Prindle, but about this stranger.

He was, however, not the type of man to wonder long. He and Vince were expecting Coley to come through that gap less than a quarter of a mile away, and this stranger, happening by, was in the way.

He pushed by Vince to the edge of the railless stoop and measured Riatt with quick and angry impatience.

"What the devil do you want, mister?"

Luke settled back in the saddle. From their action he knew these two men had been expecting someone else . . . they were obviously surprised to see him, and not pleased.

The girl, however, had uttered no sound although her rough handling by the leathery-faced Vince must have hurt. He noticed the bruise on her face, and yet the look she gave him was one of relief.

Beadle snapped his question again with thinning patience.

Temper nagged at Riatt's nerves. But it was obvious he had stumbled into something that didn't concern him, and he couched his answer accordingly.

"Just a drink, maybe—and a few words with whoever runs this store."

Vince was staring past Luke to the Pass. Irritation prodded him. He didn't want trouble with Luke, but Coley Prindle should be coming through that gap at any time. So he answered Riatt sharply and with no quarter:

"Not today, mister! Turn that nag around an' ride out of here!"

Riatt's hands were folded on his saddle. He saw that although the balding man still had his hand on the heel of his Colt, Beadle was holding his ready. It was not the time for arguments, he thought, so he nodded agreement.

"Some other time then. . . ." And he started to pull back on the reins.

He didn't see the rider behind him, who

appeared in the mouth of the Pass. But the girl did, and she reacted violently. She shoved Vince into Beadle, and her cry of warning was shrill and clear.

The rider in the Pass wheeled around and vanished. . . . Simultaneously with the girl's cry a .50-caliber slug, fired by Mel Stringer on the rim of the cliff wall, ploughed past Riatt, ricocheting off the stone building.

Luke reacted instinctively. He went out of the saddle in a twisting fall that brought him between his mount and the two men on the veranda. Vince was drawing as Luke fell. . . . Beadle, stepping away to clear his partner, levelled his Colt.

Luke's first shot smashed Vince's gun arm. The Broken Crown man fell back and into Beadle's line of fire. Ed's bullet burned across Vince's side, bringing a sharp grunt of pain, twisting him around.

Riatt was shooting up from under the neck of his mount. His next two bullets doubled Beadle.

Vince was down on his knees, his face twisted with pain. He lunged forward and tried to pick up his Colt with his left hand.

Rosalie ran between Vince and Luke, and Riatt momentarily held his fire. The girl caught the roan's trailing reins and twisted into the saddle with the lithe grace of a Sioux warrior. She had the animal turned around and lunging into a run before Luke was aware of her move.

With the protective bulk of the roan gone, he was exposed, and he moved violently, sensing the threat of the rifle on the rim. The heavy-caliber slug ploughed into the baked earth a foot behind him.

Vince had his fingers on his Colt when Luke's heel ground down on the back of his hand. The Broken Crown man gave a sharp cry and tried to bite Luke's leg. Riatt booted the gun off the stoop, dragged Vince to his feet and shoved him through the doorway at the moment another slug from Mel Stringer ripped a chunk from the worn boards at his heels.

Vince sprawled face downward inside the store; the shock of pain from his torn arm elicited a weak gasp from him. He lay still, breathing raggedly.

Riatt lingered just inside the doorway, his glance picking up the girl as she rode into the protective shadow of the Pass. He cast a quick upward look at the rim, but whoever had been shooting down at him had pulled back and was no longer in view.

The voice from behind rang flat and uncompromising: "Get back against the wall, mister. *And stay there!*"

CHAPTER FIVE

Luke realized then that there was someone else in the store beside the man he had shoved inside. He still had his Colt in his fist, and a reckless tide pulsed through him.

He threw a look over his shoulder and saw Pete Shawlee standing slack against the bar. The dark, graying man was holding a sawed-off shotgun that immediately checked the reckless temper in Riatt.

Vince Stringer hunched up and looked at Shawlee and said viciously: "Kill him, Pete!"

Shawlee shook his head. "The devil with you, Vince!" he growled, and motioned to Riatt with the shotgun. "Mister, you walk over there and lay that gun down on the table; then move back and sit down!"

Luke studied the situation and saw no percentage in defying the man. He looked entirely capable and quietly determined, and Luke had no quarrel with the man.

He walked around Vince and laid his gun on the table and stepped clear. But he stayed on his feet, turning to face Shawlee.

Peter was looking at Vince. "I told you Broken

Crown men to keep yore fightin' away from here," the storekeeper said. "When you come through North Pass you're on my territory, Vince—and don't you forget it!"

Vince lurched to his feet, clamping his fingers around his bullet-torn arm. He was in pain, and blood dripped through his fingers; despite his rage he was too hurt to utter more than a weak snarl of defiance.

Shawlee turned to Riatt. "Who are you?"

Luke shrugged. "Just a stranger who happened to ride this way at the wrong time," he said. He added evenly: "I'm not a Broken Crown man, if that helps."

Shawlee's shoulders moved in a noncommittal shrug. "Wouldn't matter any if you were." He threw a glance through the doorway. "What happened out there? Where's Ed Beadle? And Rosalie?"

"Beadle's dead," Luke answered grimly. "The girl got away, on my horse. Was she a kin of yours?"

"Not my kin," Shawlee replied. He motioned to Vince. "His."

Vince said through clenched teeth, "You're lucky you only lost yore horse, mister. Ride through North Pass an' you'll be dead before the sun sets!"

Riatt ignored him.

"Mind if I take a peek outside?" he asked

Shawlee. "The rifleman on the rim might have decided to come down and see what a bad shot he was."

Shawlee shrugged. "Take a look," he assented. He came around the bar, still holding the shotgun, picked up Luke's Colt, gave it a quick glance, then turned to Vince.

"Looks like you'll bleed to death, standing there." He turned and called to his wife: "Maria!"

At his second call a fat Mexican woman appeared in the curtained-off inner room beyond the bar. She listened impassively to Shawlee's Mexican orders and disappeared.

Luke was at the door, squinting toward the ridge. The canyon road was empty. The rim of Broken Crown showed no movement. Turning slightly, he could see Beadle's body sprawled in the dust just off the stoop, his gun still clenched in his fist.

When he turned back into the room he saw that Shawlee's wife had come back and was placing a pitcher of water, carbolic salve and strips of white cloth on the table.

Vince stood against the wall, his face beginning to show his weakness. But he shook his head as the woman turned to him.

Shawlee moved to him. "No need to be a fool, Vince. I've no quarrel with you."

Vince turned to Luke.

"Wasn't of my choosing, either," Luke replied

43

to Vince's grim stare. "I had to kill your partner . . . he was gunning for me!"

Vince moved to the chair and sagged down into it. "Ed was a fool," he admitted. "I reckon he asked for what he got."

Luke shrugged. Maria went to work on Vince, using a sharp kitchen knife to slit the sleeve to Vince's shoulder, exposing the ugly bullet hole. She worked swiftly and efficiently, as though she had patched up bullet wounds before.

When she was through she gathered up her materials and left, a silent, uncaring woman.

Shawlee looked at Vince. "You can rest up in my back room," he suggested.

Vince shook his head. He got to his feet, sucked his lips in over stubby teeth to conceal his weakness. The ingrained dirt in the creases of his face stood out plainly.

"For this I'll overlook what you said, Pete," he muttered grudgingly. "But Buck won't like it when he hears about Rosalie."

"I didn't ask her here," Shawlee replied. His voice was stiff. "I couldn't turn her out."

"Maybe Buck will make you wish you had," Vince said. He indicated the back door with his good hand. "My cayuse an' Ed's are tied up in back. If you'll give me a hand with Ed, I'll get him back to the ranch."

Riatt walked to the rear door with them. He glanced out and saw a steel-dust mare jerking

44

at her reins. Beside her was a meek-looking gray.

Luke made his choice. "Leave the steel-dust," he said shortly. "I'm riding her."

Vince turned, his eyes narrowing angrily. "That's Ed's cayuse—"

"The girl took mine," Luke cut in coldly. "A fair swap."

Vince was too weak to argue. He nodded. "A swap—"

"A temporary loan," Luke corrected grimly. "My roan is worth two of that steel-dust."

Vince shook his head. He put his hands around the pommel and tried to one-arm himself into the saddle. Luke gave him a boost. The older man settled himself, then turned the gray toward the road.

Luke walked with him to the front of the store. He knew he stood exposed to anyone watching from the rim. He caught Vince's quick glance up at the rim; then the Broken Crown man looked down at him.

"They weren't after you, mister," he repeated harshly. "They're after Coley—an' they'd be long gone now."

Vince waited while Shawlee and Luke lifted Beadle's body across the saddle in front of him. He sucked in a deep breath.

"I'm a fair man," he muttered to Luke. "Reckon Ed an' me kinda forced yore hand. But don't push yore luck too far. Don't be here when we come back!"

Luke put his back against the porch support and hooked his thumb in his cartridge belt. "I didn't come looking for trouble," he said slowly; "only for one man. I won't be here when you come back. I'll be in the Basin, looking for him."

Vince stared down at him. "Lookin' for who?"

"Lee Stringer."

The old man suddenly inhaled sharply. His eyes flared. "Lee? Then yo're—yo're—"

"Luke Riatt—Texas Ranger!"

Vince seemed to sag a little. A grudging respect mingled with the cold enmity in his eyes. He licked his lips in grim anticipation.

"We've been expectin' you," he said shortly. "I'll tell Buck yo're comin'."

Luke nodded. He watched Vince pull his gray away and send him at an easy jog toward the deep shadows of North Pass.

CHAPTER SIX

Shawlee stood framed in the doorway, the shotgun tucked under his arm. The tawny dust hung in the air behind the roan's hoofs, and the smell of it irritated his nostrils. He felt the dry sapping heat that clung like an invisible fog over the outpost and responded with the unconcern of a man who has lived with it most of his life. He stood tall and erect, eyeing Riatt with a sort of detached wonder.

Luke was occupied with his own grim thoughts. He had not wanted trouble, nor had he planned to take on Broken Crown when he had left Ysleta.

He could have wired Captain Hughes for help when he was in Ysleta, and he knew he would have had half the regiment ride with him into Broken Crown. But he had known that would not assure the capture of Lee . . . and most likely it would have provoked open war between Buck Stringer and his riders and the Rangers.

No, he had come to feel that Lee was his responsibility. . . . In some way he had failed the man, and it was now his duty to bring him back without endangering the small band of hard-riding Rangers of Company D who alone at this point in history kept order along that wild section of Texas-Mexican Border.

Now he looked toward North Pass with brooding doubts. He knew little of the Stringer clan, other than that old Buck Stringer ramrodded a wild bunch who were suspected of many things, from Border rustling to fomenting revolution across the Mexican Line. The wild and trackless country behind Broken Crown was his territory, and in it Buck Stringer's word was the only law.

Behind him Shawlee said wonderingly: "You a Ranger, mister?"

Luke turned and nodded. Standing there in the scant shade cast by the rickety wooden awning, he felt small and diminished by the towering limestone wall beyond. He also felt tired, and a vague irritation tightened his lips.

"What was the trouble here?" he asked curtly.

Shawlee's face was impassive. "Stringer trouble. Man you killed was Ed Beadle, one of the Stringer bunch. Vince is Buck Stringer's brother. They run this part of Texas."

Luke smiled harshly as he walked toward Shawlee. "They run this place, too?"

"No one runs Shawlee," the gray-headed man answered stiffly. He moved back into the comparative coolness of the store and waved to the long wooden table by the wall. "You hungry?"

Luke shrugged. "Might be, after a bottle of cold beer." He walked to the table and sat down, and

Shawlee came over with the bottle and a glass. He stood across the table, watching Riatt.

"That was Rosalie Stringer who took yore bronc," he said. "Buck Stringer's girl."

Luke poured. The news surprised him, but he was not overly interested in the pattern of trouble he had walked into. "Didn't know Buck had a daughter," he said quietly. "Heard he wasn't partial to having women on Broken Crown."

Shawlee sat down across from Luke. "Buck's first wife died right after Lee Stringer was born. He married his Mexican housekeeper. Rosalie is their daughter."

Luke frowned. "That buggy tied up outside—hers?"

Shawlee nodded. "From what I heard, she was running away with one of her father's riders—a kid named Coley Prindle."

Riatt drank his beer. It explained what he had run into here. He thought of the girl, slim and young and frightened—afraid for the man who was to have joined her there. Perhaps she had gotten back through the Pass in time to warn him. . . .

"Buck Stringer must have gotten wind of it," Shawlee continued. "Vince and Beadle got here about an hour ago. They must have had some-body up on Broken Crown ridge waiting to signal them as soon as Coley started through the Pass—"

"They treated her pretty rough," Luke

commented coldly. "Reckon Buck Stringer isn't filled with love for his girl."

Shawlee's dark face held a wooden reserve. "Buck Stringer never loved anyone in his life," he said slowly; "not even his children. Runs them with an iron fist. Until today, Lee Stringer was the only one who bucked him. Went down into Rincon town an' married an outsider, a waitress who worked in the *Cozy Corner Lunch*. Brought her back to Crown Basin. Six months later she ran off—"

Luke leaned forward, suddenly interested. "Lee was married?"

Shawlee nodded. "Girl named Milly. Ran off with a gambler named Slick Mason." He got up and walked behind his bar and returned with another bottle of beer and a glass. He poured himself a drink and pushed the bottle toward Luke. "I heard rumors old Buck Stringer was behind that—arranged it. He didn't want Lee tied to any woman."

Luke lifted the cool beer to his lips. "What happened to Lee?"

"Took it hard," Shawlee answered. "He left the Basin right after. I heard he searched for her for two years." He hesitated, his eyes dark and brooding, not looking at Luke. "Lee Stringer came through here two days ago, a changed man. He was always the best of the Stringers. He didn't have his brother's mean streak, or his father's wild temper. I asked him if he had found his wife—" Shawlee shrugged. "He didn't say a word. He left a near dead horse in my corral an' borrowed one of mine."

Luke put his glass down on the table. "He found her," he murmured, and he was thinking that he understood Lee Stringer a little better now.

Shawlee rose. He stood by the table as his wife brought Riatt a plate of enchiladas and frijoles and tortillas. "I heard Lee killed her," he said slowly. "That is true?"

Luke nodded.

Shawlee's face went wooden. He moved away toward the bar, and Luke eyed him with curiosity. "You knew Lee's wife?"

Shawlee shrugged. "Yes. It was I who wrote to Lee," he said slowly. "I thought he would—" he groped for words, and ended lamely—"not kill her."

"I'm sorry he did," Luke commented coldly. "He also killed the man she was with . . . and stole twenty thousand dollars he was supposed to help guard."

Shawlee's eyes reflected a bitter amazement. "He used to come here often before he went away. He was different from the other Stringers."

How different? Luke thought coldly. Lee was a Stringer, brought up in an atmosphere of violence. When the time came he had reacted like a Stringer.

He ate without much hunger, although he had not eaten since early morning. Shawlee brooded behind his bar—he seemed to be taking the responsibility for Milly's death as his own.

The shadows of Broken Crown stretched far down the slant of tawny earth toward Tortilla Flats—no breeze stirred the heat of the dying afternoon.

Riatt got up, left money on the table by his plate and walked to the door. He eyed the towering wall with a brooding regard as he slowly took out his Ranger badge and as slowly pinned it to his dusty shirt.

There was no longer need to hide the fact that he was a Ranger. Lee must have guessed he'd come after him . . . and when Vince got back Buck Stringer would know.

Shawlee joined him. The dark-faced man eyed the symbol of Border authority on Luke's shirt—a lone star circled with a gleaming band of silver. It seemed out of place in that country, that symbol of law and order—a worthless bit of bright metal. But the tall, wide-shouldered man with the grave face gave it stature—almost, Shawlee hesitated, gave it meaning!

Again he groped for words. "You are a brave man, Mister Riatt. But if you value your life, stay out of Crown Basin!"

Luke didn't answer him. He only half heard Shawlee; he was thinking of what lay beyond the barrier. He was thinking, too, of the frightened girl who had taken his horse.

"Men come and go through North Pass," Shawlee muttered. He seemed to be talking mostly for himself. "They pause here for a beer— sometimes to eat. I hear many things. Buck Stringer has something big planned; something to do with Cordero, the Mexican bandit."

Luke turned to look at him, caught by some vague portent in Shawlee's tone. "How big?" he asked bluntly.

The other shrugged. "That I do not know. But whatever it is, he will not let you interfere. If you ride through that Pass they'll kill you!"

"They'll try," Luke amended grimly. He smiled then, and the harsh planes of his face softened. He put out his hand. "Thanks for everything, Shawlee. But it's time I was riding."

Shawlee watched him mount the steel-dust Vince had been forced to leave behind. He answered Luke's brief wave. Of all the men who had come and gone in the years since he had settled there, he had met none like this one. Something bitter put a bad taste in his mouth—a premonition. Some day soon he would hear the news from some tight-lipped Broken Crown rider . . . Luke Riatt was dead!

He turned and went slowly back into the store. . . .

CHAPTER SEVEN

Lee Stringer stared moodily from the veranda of the ranchhouse. Around him were flimsily built outbuildings, *ramadas* mostly, designed to protect from the brutal Border sun and little more. Even the ranchhouse, sprawling and ugly, had not been built with an eye toward permanency. Broken Crown was a camp which could be burned out without impairing the power of Buck Stringer or greatly inconveniencing him.

As far as Lee could see the land was bare and barren, breaking against the high mesa country which hid the canyon cut of the Rio Grande. It was a grim and uninhabited stretch of Texas, tenanted only by fugitives and scum of both Border countries.

Lee Stringer stood against the bleached porch support and watched the sun go down over the ragged hills. He had not shaved in days, and his hair was long and shaggy on the back of his neck. He seemed caught in a miasma of inactivity—it was as though he could not will even the simplest act. From the day he had killed Slick Mason and the girl who had been his wife, Lee had lived as in a bad dream. He had fled here where he had been born, not knowing why, impelled by some obscure homing instinct.

Deep inside him he knew it had been a mistake to come back here. The things which had driven him from Broken Crown were still here, and the memories of the woman he had killed were here, too. He felt mortally sick deep down inside him, and he knew he lacked the will to recover.

He shaped himself a cigaret from habit, and over the match flame he studied the far barrier of Broken Crown. Luke would be coming from that direction, he knew, and a dark and brooding impulse toward destruction welcomed the thought.

The screen door slammed behind him, and his father and a stumpy, ragged Mexican came outside. The Mexican wore a cartridge bandolier across his shoulder and carried an ancient carbine in his hand—he was mostly Yaqui, stolid, still overwhelmed by the power of the weapon he owned. He was a member of Cordero's ragged rebel army which, Lee knew, was nothing more than a motley raiding crew.

The Mexican cast a dark, arrogant look at Lee as he went down the steps, caught up the trailing reins of his shaggy pony and rode away.

Buck Stringer watched him go, then moved to his youngest son's side. Buck was not a big man, but he gave the impression of bigness. He stood several inches shorter than Lee, but he was half again as broad. There was a thick, ponderous, invincible quality in this mahogany-hued man with the iron-gray mustache, pale blue eyes and blunt, scarred chin, and it made an impression on even a casual acquaintance.

Buck Stringer had come into Broken Crown Basin at the age of twenty-two—he had had a price on his head even then. He had been riding with Quantrill from the age of sixteen, and he had learned to kill early. In that back border country of vast distances, canyon breaks and mesas, he had found what he wanted.

He was a generous man as long as he was obeyed. Money meant little to him, except that he gloried in its acquisition and the power money gave him. Even his sons didn't know how much money he had locked away in the iron safe in his cubbyhole office.

But he paid wages to twenty riders, and his intrigues reached into a dozen border towns and into Chihuahua. Beyond Broken Crown he was the only law, and Texas be hanged!

Standing beside his son, he sensed what was eating Lee. His voice had a reproving note. "You ain't afraid of him are yuh, son?"

Lee didn't look at him. The question got no rise from him. It wasn't fear he felt; only an implacable certainty. "He'll come," he muttered. "I know Luke Riatt!"

"Bah!" His father spat into the dust. "I'll wager a hundred to one that Ranger won't show his face past North Gap. Shore, I know what you said about him . . . I heard other stories, too. But he ain't fool enough to come into Crown Basin to try to arrest my own son!"

A faint smile lifted the corners of Lee's mouth. He reached inside his pocket and took out a silver dollar and placed it on the veranda railing. "It's a bet," he said softly.

Anger flared harshly in Buck's pale eyes. "What in blazes has gotten into you, son? Yuh useta be near as hard as Mel before yuh went away. Even figgered yuh was smart to join the Rangers. But I never knew any man big enough to scare yuh!"

"He ain't that big . . . and I ain't exactly scared, Pa," Lee said finally. "But Luke will be showing up. It's not him that's worrying me—it's me. I don't know what I'll do when Luke rides in here."

Buck Stringer was not a sensitive man, and he missed Lee's point entirely. "You won't have to do anythin'," he growled contemptuously. "Mel will take care of him. I don't have time to bother with any crazy badge-toter who thinks his tin badge means anything in my country!"

Lee's eyes held a thin amusement, a surface reaction to his father's blind confidence. "If Mel draws on Luke Riatt," he said flatly, "you'll bury him. Mel's fast—but not that fast!"

Buck scowled. "You believe that, eh?"

"I worked with him," Lee reminded bitterly. "I know how good Luke is."

Lee's dull voice stirred up the latent violence that always lay just below the surface in Buck Stringer. "You've shore gone soft since yuh left, ever since Milly left yuh to run off with that slick-talkin' gamblin' fella." The older man's prodding voice baited his son. "I warned yuh not to marry her. You could have had her anyway if yuh wanted her that bad—"

Lee swung. His fist smashed into Buck's mouth, staggering the heavier man. The motion was a reaction, as though his father had prodded a nerve end. He saw Buck's rough features break into a blood-streaked smile. Then the older man backhanded him across the face, spilling him over the low railing. . . .

Lee Stringer lay on the hot ground, spitting blood. His anger had left him as quickly as it had flared up . . . there was no fight in him now.

"Get up!" Buck challenged harshly, standing against the railing. *"Get up!"* As Lee remained on the ground: "Haven't you even got guts enough to back up what yuh started?"

Lee got to his feet and brushed dirt from his clothes. He did it mechanically. A wicked light burned in Buck's eyes as his hands fisted. He knew he could beat his son into the dust, and he was welcoming the chance.

Lee drew the back of his hand across his cut lips. "Sorry," he apologized thickly.

Buck's heavy shoulders quivered in disappointment. He wanted to break his son out of the dark, unfathomable mood he seemed to be in. "What in the devil are yuh sorry about?" he blazed. "About what I said concerning yore wife?"

"She's dead," Lee said tonelessly. "Leave her be."

"You oughta be glad yo're rid of her," his father snapped harshly.

Lee's eyes were dead. "Maybe," he muttered, and walked past his father into the house.

Buck Stringer stood with clenched fists, glaring at the screen door. He couldn't understand what was bothering Lee. His woman had run out on him—in his code she deserved killing. That he had arranged and abetted it did not in the least bother him.

But it riled him that he couldn't reach his son, and it irked him even more to feel that Lee was afraid of a man. Luke Riatt! He snorted. He had trampled too many reputations to be impressed by this lone wolf Ranger. If Riatt was fool enough to show his face past the rim of Broken Crown, he'd be shown little mercy.

He drew a deep breath and unclenched his hands and put his gaze on the dark, ragged barrier rimming the Basin. The tides of his anger still engulfed him.

59

They should be showing up with Rosalie soon. He had little doubt but that they had overtaken his daughter; he wondered maliciously what fate Mel had meted out to Coley Prindle.

Not that he cared about the dark, shy girl he had fathered; it was her defiance of him that bothered him.

Buck Stringer ruled Broken Crown, from his sons and daughter to the most hardened rider—and no man left his employ without Buck's consent. There was arrogance in this man, and a hungering need. . . .

Somewhere by the corrals a man shouted, and Buck's attention was drawn to the rider showing up on the trail beyond. Even in the distance he recognized his brother's stooped figure—his eyes narrowed on the limp body across Vince's saddle.

Men drifted out of the bunkhouse across the yard to stare curiously. A few began to run toward the rider.

Buck waited, an unbelieving scowl darkening his features. In the hot stillness the roan's tired hoofs rang on the hard ground with implacable finality.

Vince shook off all offers of help. He rode up to where Buck waited, his teeth sucked in against his bloodless lips. He had something to tell his brother before the weakness he had been fighting engulfed him.

"Rosalie got away. Mel an' Slim are trailin' her an' Coley. They're in the Basin somewhere—"

Buck's voice cut brutally across his brother's story. "Never mind Rosalie. What happened to you an' Ed? Did Coley—?"

Vince sneered. He had a good deal of his brother's arrogance, but not his untempered violence. "Never got to see Coley." He licked his lips. "Me an' Beadle tied into a ring-dinger, Buck: a Ranger named Luke Riatt." He saw the harsh shock of surprise go through Buck Stringer, and he shook his head. "He's comin' up here, Buck—a bad man to tangle with—"

He was trying to talk as he dismounted. Blackness washed up over him as he unhooked a leg from the stirrup and swung it over his saddle. He slid out and down, and Buck caught him as he fell. . . .

CHAPTER EIGHT

Luke Riatt left Shawlee's Store at sundown. He rode into the deep shadows of North Pass, a tall alert man who did not entirely trust the quiet peace of this narrow gorge or the still heights above him.

The Stringer brand, a Broken Crown, was burned into the hind quarter of the steel-dust. It was a symbol of old Buck Stringer's defiance of Texas law.

The floor of the canyon lifted and wound through the gorge, emerging finally along the flank of the first of the Tombstones, naked spires of rock that dotted the Basin.

There were few corners of Texas that were alien to the big Ranger, but this broken land that stretched out ahead of him, spilling across the border into Chihuahua, was new to Riatt.

He had no other plan except to ride into Buck's camp for Lee Stringer—he was riding a hunch that his bluff might work. The badge on his shirt gave testimony to the weight of the Texas Rangers behind him—in most sections of Texas it gave men pause. But he wasn't sure that Buck Stringer would be impressed.

It was on Lee Stringer that Riatt pinned his hopes. The man had once been a Ranger—some of it might have rubbed off on him. . . .

The steel-dust snorted softly and quickened her pace, and Luke smiled thinly as he gave her her head. There was no visible trail to Broken Crown—but the steel-dust knew the way.

Night sucked the last vestige of day from the gullied land. Stars pricked the velvet blackness of the arching sky, some of them so low they seemed yellow beacons on the dark and distant hills.

The Ranger drifted with the steel-dust, not pushing it. He missed his roan's rhythmic stride, the animal's awareness. The steel-dust was a stranger to him, and they both knew it.

The Broken Crown bronc slid down a crumbly bank and turned south to follow the course of an old stream bed gleaming white under the stars. Luke pulled the animal in toward the bank. A rider could be easily spotted against the pale sand. . . .

The distant slam of a six-gun brought him up in the saddle. The shots came from somewhere ahead, somewhat smothered by the dark bulk of a rise which forced the old stream bed into a wide bend. Two shots . . . it might have been three . . . Luke wasn't sure. The last two could have been so close together as to sound like one.

They came from around the bend, and a hard caution rode Luke. He dismounted and tied the steel-dust to a bush and waited, frowning, remembering that his movements could have been watched from the time he left Shawlee's Store.

Might be the gents who signaled from the rim caught up with the girl and Coley Prindle, he thought, and regret left its rue in him. He had hoped Rosalie Stringer would manage to get away. . . .

He left the shadows of the bank and broke for the far side of the stream bed, moving fast. He was in deep shadows again when the girl screamed! It lifted the hackles on his neck.

Luke Riatt turned and headed directly for the sound, a grim urgency driving him. He skirted the shouldering hill and suddenly paused to eye the campfire in the dark gully below.

The girl screamed again. He could see her just beyond the fire, standing by a figure slumped against the bank. She was covering her face with her hands. . . .

A lean, wiry individual stood closer to the fire. His saddle lay on the sand a few feet away and his rifle rested across it. The girl now started to back away from the slumped figure, and the slim man grabbed her, spun her around and slapped her. She staggered and sank down, still hiding her face in her hands.

Luke started down the slope. He walked with the soft tread of a hunting cat, his face dark and expressionless.

In the shadows beyond the fire, horses moved. The Ranger caught the sheen of his roan's coat; he saw the animal suddenly raise his head and look toward the slope. A whinny fluttered in the roan's throat.

The slim man whirled around, his glance probing the gully shadows. He took a long stride toward his rifle just as Luke reached the outer edge of the fire.

"Let it lay, *compadre*!" Luke warned harshly.

Slim Meeker froze. He was wearing a belt gun, and there was a knife in a sheath at his side. He kept his hands away from them, a cold, expressionless look in his eyes.

The girl remained kneeling, her face in her hands.

Luke came into the firelight. He could see the slumped figure against the bank now; the body of what had once been a slim, curly-haired man. Coley Prindle, he thought bleakly. The man had paid with uncalled for violence for his attentions to Buck Stringer's daughter. He had been shot twice in the chest; then his throat had been cut. . . .

The girl rocked softly and moaned. A sickening anger blurred Luke's gaze as he took in the naked cruelty of his scene.

He stepped up to the Broken Crown man, shoved him roughly around, reached for his holstered Colt and tossed it into the darkness. Meeker stood still under the rough handling . . . he seemed to sense the grim violence in the Ranger.

Even when Riatt slipped the knife from its sheath he made no move. The Ranger glanced at the clean blade. . . .

The voice close behind Luke was sibilantly cruel. "Not his, Ranger. Mine. I cut Prindle's throat. Meeker ain't got the stomach for it!"

Riatt was holding Meeker's knife in his right hand, but he knew he'd be dead before he could use it. Meeker grinned sourly as he edged away from Luke. And a realization of how neatly he had been trapped sickened Riatt.

The man behind him moved with the slithering tread of an Apache. There was an Apache's flat cruelty in the voice that said: "Welcome to the Tombstones, Ranger."

Luke whirled. He had Meeker's knife in his hand, and he slipped it behind him, hoping more to distract his ambusher than to score a hit. The palmed Colt smashed against the back of his head, driving him forward into a leaping, fiery blackness. . . .

Mel Stringer chuckled. He was a wolf of a man standing over Riatt, his enormous shoulders humped in readiness. He was an ugly man with light gray eyes in a dark face. He walked and looked like a broncho Apache; he wore moccasins and the tails of his dirty cotton shirt hung out over his greasy pants. He wore his belt guns over the shirttail.

"Spotted him crossin' the arroyo around the bend," he told Slim. "Saw him leave Vince's steel-dust hitched to a bush 'bout a half-mile from here. Go git it. I'll keep him company until yuh git back."

Slim nodded. He hauled his saddle into the shadows and a few minutes later was riding up the arroyo.

Mel stood over Luke, waiting with stolid patience. The fire died down, and the shadows hid Prindle's body. Mel's sister made no sound, and he ignored her, as though she didn't exist. He waited with his gun cocked until Meeker showed up, riding his dun and leading the steel-dust.

The Ranger stirred. He rolled over and looked up at the man standing above him, and at first his pained gaze made out only distorted shadows. He set his teeth against the throbbing in his head and waited for his eyes to clear. . . .

"So yo're Luke Riatt," Mel sneered, "the Ranger who's got my brother Lee shakin' in his boots?" He spat in Luke's face. "Well, I'm gonna whittle yuh down to size an' hang yore hide out to dry on the corral fence. I'll show Lee what he's been runnin' from!"

Luke slowly wiped his face. He got to his feet and faced the man, a cold and dispassionate anger held in check by the gun in Mel's fist.

Meeker slid out of the saddle and came up behind the Ranger. He was a cautious man and he moved quickly; he had Luke's Peacemaker Colt before Luke realized it had been taken from him.

"Feel easier with him defanged, Mel," Slim said. He glanced at Prindle's body. "What do you want to do with *him?*"

"Leave him to the coyotes," Mel growled. "Bring the other hosses. We've done what we came for. An' got ourselves a prize, too."

While Meeker headed for the horses tied up in the shadows beyond the dying fire, Mel walked over to where his half-sister kneeled. She cringed as he loomed over her. He grabbed her by the hair with his left hand and jerked her to her feet.

"I oughta do to you what I done to him," he growled, motioning to Coley's body.

A deep, futile hate burned in Rosalie's eyes. But there was no fight in her. Watching, Luke felt a compassion for her which fanned his helpless anger.

Meeker came back, leading Goldy and another saddled mount. "Coley's gray is wind broke," he announced. "Want him along?"

Mel scowled. "Can't stand a hoss I have to baby," he snarled. He stepped into the brush beyond the fire. The report of his Colt made a heavy sound in the night.

He came back, the muzzle of his Colt leaking smoke. He backed his curt order with it. "You'll ride my dun, Ranger. I got a fancy for that big roan stud of yores."

Luke hesitated. Mel's hammer cocked; there was short patience in the man. "Git aboard, Ranger! Or else I'll be bringin' my brother a dead lawman for a present!"

The dun snorted and jerked as Luke took the reins from Meeker. He felt a heavy pounding in his head as he put his foot in the stirrup and heaved himself up.

The dun backed away from Meeker, who was settling in the saddle of his own mount. Rosalie was a still, small figure on the steel-dust.

Mel Stringer walked to Riatt's big roan. The animal turned to eye the stranger with a suspicious stare.

Mel caught the roan's reins and started to swing up to the saddle. Luke's sudden whistle caught him by surprise. The seemingly docile stallion whirled and reared up on its hind legs, its forefeet slashing out. Mel was sent sprawling. The roan lunged into the shadows.

Mel Stringer came to his feet, cursing; his hand jumped to his holster gun. He was clearing leather when Luke sent the dun hurtling into the killer.

Mel's shot went wild as he was spun around and sent staggering again. Riatt made a break for it. He dug his heels into the dun's sides, and the animal lunged ahead. He was beyond Mel when the hump-shouldered man's Colt roared.

The dun went down, shot through the head. Riatt fell free. He scrambled to his feet and suddenly stopped as Meeker rode his cayuse in front of him.

"Hold it, Ranger!" the Broken Crown rider snapped. "You ain't goin' anywhere!"

Mel Stringer came up, his ugly face twisted with a wild snarl. "So yuh managed to get that big roan of yores free! Made me kill my own hoss! Fixed it so one of us has to walk, eh—a real long walk, Ranger. Now guess just who it's gonna be!"

Luke shrugged. He had made his try—he was lucky he was still alive.

"Ride up with Rosalie," Mel told Meeker. "I'll ride yore bronc."

Meeker switched mounts. Mel settled himself in the saddle, shook out a loop and flipped it expertly over Riatt, jerking it tight. "Let's go," he chuckled, and kicked his animal into a run.

CHAPTER NINE

Broken Crown was asleep when Luke Riatt stumbled into the big yard behind Mel Stringer. He had run most of the way and been dragged part of the way, and only an iron, unbeatable will kept him on his feet now.

Mel jerked his bronc to a stop before the darkened ranchhouse. His Colt leaped out, and he fired three shots into the air, following them with a wild rebel yell.

The bunkhouse door creaked and a long-john-clad figure cradling a Winchester loomed up in the aperture. Mel whirled and sent a shot crashing over the bunkhouse. His voice boomed triumphantly. "Pile out, yuh ear-poundin' mavericks! I brung home the prize bacon!"

A light glowed against the ranchhouse windows, and then Buck Stringer yanked the door open and strode outside. He was in bare feet and under-wear. He had a hat jammed on his head, and he held a cocked Colt in his big fist. He came down into the yard, surveyed the starlit figures and snapped with harsh impatience, "You gone loco, son?"

Mel turned to him. "Where's Lee, Paw? I brung

him a present." His tone was gleeful. "I brung him thet Ranger he's been scairt of!"

Buck Stringer stiffened. He peered at the tall figure at the end of Mel's rope.

"Luke Riatt?"

"Yup. Tin badge an' all!"

Buck grunted. "Wal, I'll be jiggered! Roped an' hog-tied—" He laughed raucously. "Lee!" he bellowed. "Come out here! You, too, Vince!"

Mel slid out of the saddle. "Took him without much fuss, Paw!" he boasted. "Knew he was comin', so when we run Coley an' Rosalie down, we set a trap for him. He walked right into it like some tenderfoot, Paw!"

Buck came down into the yard. "Untie him," he told Mel. "I want a good look at the Ranger who's got half the badmen in Texas huntin' for cover!"

Mel grunted. He walked up behind the Ranger and drew his sheath knife. He wasn't expecting trouble from this man he had run ragged. He slid the sharp edge over Luke's thongs and cut them loose.

The miles of dragging humiliation had built up a vicious driving rage in the big Ranger that blinded him now to the consequences of what he was about to do. He waited until he felt his arms loosen; then he pivoted, driving his right hand into Mel's face.

Mel was caught flat-footed, knife in hand. Luke's fist smashed his mouth. He staggered back, and Luke chopped down with the edge of his palm against Mel's knife arm just above the wrist.

Mel's lips sucked in sharply against loosened teeth. He dropped the knife and reached for his holstered Colt with his other hand.

Luke's right hand caught him on the side of his heavy jaw. The force of the blow spun Mel around, and the Ranger's left, slashing downward with the weight of Luke's shoulders behind it, crumpled the hump-shouldered killer. He sagged and fell on his knees and then slumped forward, his forehead bumping against the hard earth.

Meeker had one of Luke's Colts in his hand and was cocking it. Buck's voice stopped him.

"I'll take care of him, Slim!"

The Broken Crown boss moved toward Luke, an incongruous figure who managed to convey grim authority despite his appearance. He paused by Mel's unconscious figure and looked at Riatt, who was sucking in great gulps of air. His thick lips quirked in a grudging smile.

"So yo're Luke Riatt? Mebbe there's somethin' to yore rep after all."

Riatt steadied himself. His whole body ached, and the pain over his eyes was sharp now, pounding. He massaged his bruised knuckles, his voice cold, demanding.

"I've come for Lee Stringer, Buck. I think you know why."

Buck nodded. "Shore I know why. But I don't

think it's anybody's business but ours, Ranger. The man my son killed wasn't worth the slugs used on him!"

"And the woman?"

"She was his wife. She was no good."

"That's not for you or Lee to decide," Luke said tersely. "He'll have to stand trial."

"No, Luke!" Lee's voice was flat. He was standing on the porch, a shadowy, lean figure. "I'm not going back with you!"

The Ranger faced the man he had come for. He was unarmed, surrounded by hostile men. But he wore his badge on his shirt and he had the might of Texas behind him.

"You swore an oath once," he reminded Lee, "to uphold law and order in Texas."

"To the devil with Texas!" Lee cried. His voice had a toneless quality. "I'm not leaving here!"

Between Buck and Riatt, Mel moved. He came to his hands and knees and shook his head like a dog. Then he lurched up to his feet, staggered against Buck's solid bulk and whirled to face Luke, his right hand jerking at his holstered Colt.

Buck Stringer caught his arm and whirled him around. "I'm handlin' this," he growled. "Keep that gun pouched! I want Riatt alive!"

Mel wiped his bloody mouth. "Don't stop me, Paw! No man kin hit me like that an' get away with it!"

"I want him alive, I said!" Buck snapped. "If

you think yo're man enough to take it outta his hide, give me yore guns!"

Mel spat blood into the night. He unbuckled his gun belts and handed them to Buck, who passed them on to the man next to him. "Make it fast," Buck growled to his son. "We got work to do in the mornin'!"

The Broken Crown men pressed around them, making a tight, silent ring. From the porch Lee Stringer watched with cold detachment.

Win or lose, Riatt knew, he'd never be allowed to leave there alive. He realized he had misjudged Lee Stringer, as he had underrated the stories he had heard about this Broken Crown bunch.

He turned to face Mel squarely, and there was no spring left in his bruised, tired frame; only a bitter determination to make Mel Stringer regret his words. . . .

Someone shoved Riatt from behind, and he staggered into Mel as the hump-shouldered man swung for Luke's face. The blow landed high on the Ranger's cheek, spinning him around. Mel closed in, driving his knee for Luke's groin.

Riatt twisted and caught the knee against his hip. He pushed the heel of his left hand out hard and caught Mel under the ear. Mel's head snapped back and Riatt crowded him, knowing he'd have to end this fast or take the beating of his life. He didn't have the stamina to make a fight of it.

He drove a hard right into Mel's midsection and caught the sagging man with an uppercut that made Mel's teeth click together. Mel's knees gave way, and the Ranger started a right for Mel's face.

A heavy blow against the back of Luke's neck sent him staggering against Mel. He caught hold of the cursing man and hung on, trying to fight the blackness before his eyes.

Buck's voice sounded from far away. "Reckon you need a little help, son. Give him his beatin' so we can all turn in for the night!"

Riatt tried to push Mel away. He felt rough hands close on his arm, pull him back, lock his hands in a helpless position behind him. Buck's sour voice rasped in his ear.

"Come on, son—get it over with!"

Mel's dark, bloody face loomed up before Luke. There was no sense of fair play here; only a cold and ugly brutality.

Mel Stringer used all his strength on the Ranger. He lashed out at Luke with a cruelty that finally brought a muffled, tortured cry from Lee Stringer.

"That's enough, Mel! *That's enough!*"

Buck turned to stare at the shadowy figure of his son on the porch. He caught the glint of a drawn gun in Lee's hand, and his breath was sharp in his throat; he shook his head in grim disbelief.

Mel turned to face his brother, a distorted, inhuman look on his bruised, bleeding face.

"Kill him if you have to!" Lee said thickly. "But do it quick—not like an Injun!"

Mel spat blood in snarling defiance to his brother. "Stay out of this, you snivelin'—"

Buck Stringer let Riatt go, and as the Ranger sagged unconscious to the ground he turned and back-handed Mel across the mouth. Then he walked to the porch, a ponderous, grim man, and yanked the Colt from Lee's fist.

"That's enough from both of you!" he snarled. "If you've gone that soft, Lee, get back into the house! Stay out of this!" He turned to Mel, who was eyeing him with sullen rebellion. "You, too. Get inside an' get that blood washed off. An' remember—what that Ranger just did to you I kin do twice as good. Now get out of my way!"

He waited until Mel stumbled past him, into the house. Then he turned to Slim, who was standing beside the steel-dust.

"Get those leg irons from the blacksmith shop. Anders," he addressed the man standing next to Meeker, "you an' Bigfoot carry this badge toter into the bunkhouse. See that he is chained to one of the empty racks. I want to see him there in the mornin'!"

Rosalie Stringer remained slumped in the saddle of the steel-dust. If she had witnessed anything that had gone on that night, she gave no evidence of it. She seemed to be in a trance.

Buck reached up and pulled her out of the

saddle. "Tina!" he shouted. "Come out here!"

A dumpy figure with coarse black hair in two pigtails came out to the porch.

Buck pulled his daughter to her feet and slapped her hard. "Next time you try to run away," he warned her flatly, "I'll kill you!"

Rosalie lifted a hand to her face. Buck shoved her toward the house. "Take this female whelp of yores, Tina," he snarled, "an' give her a hidin'! An' if she runs away again I'll kill both of you!"

The Broken Crown riders went back into the bunkhouse, trailing Bigfoot and Anders as they carried the unconscious Ranger. The steel-dust drifted toward the corral, joining Mel's animal against the pole bars.

Buck Stringer stood alone in the trampled yard, a big, hard man, conscious of the authority he wielded.

"You came at the right time, Riatt," he muttered.

He was thinking of Cordero, the Mexican bandit chief across the Mexican Border. He had promised Cordero guns and money—but all the stolid, arrogant Mexican had said was, "Maybe."

Guns and money had not been enough to swing Cordero into making the deal Buck Stringer wanted. But he knew the Mexican bandit chief . . . and he knew how much Cordero wanted the big Ranger in the bunkhouse.

"Just in time," he repeated, and felt an immense satisfaction with the night's happenings.

CHAPTER TEN

The flat light of the early sun filtered through the dirty bunkhouse window and crept down the side of the bunk where Riatt lay. There was movement in the long room as men stirred and dressed, accompanied by morning oaths, growls and mutters of bad temper.

Luke lay on his back, both his legs chained to the uprights at the foot of his bunk. His face ached as he moved his split lips. He was still fully dressed, in torn and dirty clothes, and his ribs pained him as he shifted his bruised, aching body.

He lay still, staring up at the ceiling, amazed that he was still in one piece. He had taken worse beatings, he thought philosophically, but the viciousness of the Stringers brought a bleak light to his yellow-green eyes.

He had seen with what utter cruelty Mel Stringer had treated his half-sister—he had an understanding now of why she had tried to run off with the unfortunate Coley Prindle.

He could understand what had driven Lee Stringer from the Tombstones. Of Milly Stringer, Lee's wife, he knew nothing. In the short time he had known Lee the renegade Ranger had never spoken of her.

But this ranch was no place for women. They did not fit in it, nor, he was to learn, did they leave their mark on it. There was no graciousness about the place. Tina Stringer, if she had ever entertained any desires to lend her touch to Broken Crown, had long ago been discouraged.

It was a man's ranch, rough, dirty and strictly utilitarian.

Luke Riatt thought of Captain Hughes, waiting for word from him. He knew the Ranger Captain had meant it when he had told Luke that if he didn't hear from him within ten days he'd take Company D into Crown Basin.

"You look like you fell in front of a stampede," a voice greeted Luke cheerfully.

Luke turned his head and watched a tall, ungainly figure hunker down beside him. The man wore a mismatched suit, dark gray coat and blue trousers which, though frayed, were neat and pressed. He was older than most of the men Luke had observed in the bunkhouse, with a thin, scholarly face and an apologetic smile. He carried a spectacle case in his breast pocket, and the marks left by the steel rims were deep across the bridge of his thin, hooked nose.

He studied Luke through watery blue eyes. "Thought I'd have to patch you up some, when

Mel drew a gun on you last night. Buck stopped him just in time."

The Ranger digested this bit of news. "You handy with arnica and bandages?"

"Probably do more patching up of knife wounds, bullet holes and assorted cussedness on Broken Crown than the average town doc," he said. He sniffed good-naturedly. "So you're the great Luke Riatt, Captain Hughes' ace trouble-shooter?"

Luke grinned sourly. "Don't feel great at all, fella," he said honestly. He wondered what the man's game was. The others had left him alone, disregarding him entirely or eyeing him with surly hostility.

"I'm Smith," the other said. He shifted his weight on his heels. "Been called 'Sawbones' Smith so long I've almost forgotten my real name. Was christened Frank Bonner. But that was a long time ago, back in Scranton, Pennsylvania."

He seemed cheerful and garrulous, and Luke listened idly. It helped him forget his bruised body, his helplessness. Smith kept talking even when the clanging of the breakfast triangle outside emptied the bunkhouse. He waited until the last man had stomped out; then his face turned grave and his voice urgent.

"I haven't got much time, Ranger. But I'm here to help you. I'm riding down to Shawlee's Store today. If you've got a message you want to send back to Ranger headquarters, give it to me. I'll see that it gets off."

Luke sat up on his bunk. The effort caused a spasm of pain to cross his bruised face.

"A message?" he repeated suspiciously.

Sawbones Smith shrugged. "I've wanted to get back at Buck Stringer for years," he said harshly. "But no man or woman leaves Broken Crown without Buck's say-so." He eyed Luke closely, his lips pursing. "They're going to kill you, Ranger. Ain't nothing I can do to help. Buck's going to turn you over to the Cordero brothers. He's sent Myers across the Border to arrange things."

"Why are you telling me?" Luke asked.

Smith glanced around the empty bunkhouse and instinctively lowered his voice. "If the Rangers were to surprise the Corderos on this side of the river, Ranger, with the Broken Crown bunch . . ." He left the sentence hang in the empty room and rubbed his hands in a nervous gesture. "I can't help you, Ranger," he muttered. "But if I could get even with Buck Stringer—"

Luke's voice interrupted him. "You sure you can get my letter mailed?"

Smith nodded. "I'm riding down to Shawlee's with Anders to pick up the buggy Rosalie left down there. Pete's a friend of mine . . . and he doesn't like Buck any better than I do!"

Luke hesitated. If he sent a note to Hughes, he

knew all of Company D would come a-running. But a nagging suspicion held him. Somehow it was all too pat—

"Sure," he said finally. "I'll write a note to Captain Hughes."

Smith nodded. "I'll get pencil and paper." He straightened and hurried to his bunk. He took notepaper, envelope and a stub of a pencil from a small tin box which he kept locked and gave them to Luke.

Luke grinned through swollen lips. He had nothing to lose if he worded the message carefully. If it got through to Captain Hughes, he would be warned. But if Smith was part of a trap Buck had planned, the message he was about to write would be of no use to them.

He told Captain Hughes what had happened to him. He mentioned his belief that Buck Stringer was planning a raid on the Border towns below the Broken Crown rim with the help of the Cordero brothers and their rebel band; that whatever was planned was due to come off soon.

He put all this in code and handed it to Smith and watched the man's face as he read it.

Smith glanced at the unintelligible message with only brief interest. He grinned and folded the message and tucked it away in his breast pocket. His manner changed.

Luke lunged for him. But Smith backed away, grinning. "The great Luke Riatt!" he mocked.

"Heck, you been outsmarted ever since you came through Broken Crown!"

He was still chuckling as he left.

Twenty minutes later Mel Stringer and a hard-faced blond kid came into the bunkhouse. Mel stood by the door, a Colt in his hand, while the kid unlocked the iron bands around Luke's ankles.

"If yuh can walk, get up an' come out!" he growled. He slouched like some lobo against the framing, his hat pulled low over his bruised, ugly face.

Luke swung his legs over the side of the bunk and was mildly surprised to find he could walk. He had to use an iron will to control his facial muscles so as not to reveal the pain which racked his body.

He walked down the length of the bunkhouse, followed by the blond, tough-faced kid. Mel eased away from the door and let Luke by; there was a sullen, contained expression on his face. He had been badly humiliated by the Ranger in front of Broken Crown's crew last night, and he wouldn't easily forget it.

Luke stepped out into the sunlit yard, his eyes squinting against the early morning brightness. He put his narrowed glance over the sprawling spread, which he now saw was backed by a low sand hill just behind the ranchhouse. Corrals and sheds staggered haphazardly away from the main house, and he saw at least a dozen men moving about.

Mel growled: "Paw wants to see yuh. In the house."

Luke walked across the yard. The blond kid hung back by the bunkhouse, waiting. Suddenly he called out: "Mel—look! Up the hill—"

Mel Stringer stopped in mid-stride. Just ahead of him Riatt raised his glance and gave a quick start.

His roan had just come into sight on the hill above the house. A big animal, it was still saddled, reins trailing. He stood outlined against the brightness of the southern sky, a magnificent animal, watching. . . .

Mel's Colt lifted, then dropped. The range was too far for a hand gun. He turned and yelled to the blond kid. "I'll pay a thousand dollars to the man who brings that roan horse in!"

The kid started to run toward the corral. Another rider, just coming out of the saddle shed, heard Mel's offer and started back for his saddle.

Riatt lifted his hand, then dropped it sharply down by his side. The big roan wheeled at the signal and disappeared.

Buck Stringer was waiting for the Ranger in the big dining room. He sat at the head of a massive oak table whose surface was devoid of any covering. The table top was spur-scoured,

85

cigaret-burned, coffee- and grease-stained. His breakfast plate was aside, and as Luke entered he was wiping his egg-stained lips with the back of his sleeve.

He looked up as Luke entered, followed by Mel. He took a long, noisy drag from his coffee mug, then settled back and drew a crooked Mexican cheroot from his pocket.

Lee Stringer sat on his father's right. The renegade Ranger was smoking a cigaret in silent, brooding thought—most of his food was on his plate, untouched.

Buck lighted up, blew a cloud of blue-gray smoke expansively toward Luke and waved grandiosely toward a chair. "Sit down, Riatt," he invited pleasantly. "I'll have my gal bring you some chow."

Mel slouched past Riatt and sank into a chair across from his brother. He looked down into his coffee mug, an angry, resentful figure.

Luke paid brief attention to the man who called himself Sawbones Smith. The man was sitting next to Buck, on his left—he rolled a matchstick around between his lips. He was wearing spectacles and working on a piece of notepaper, pausing to study the message Luke had written out and handed to him.

A sinking feeling took hold of the big Ranger. He had purposely worded his message so that Captain Hughes would be warned, and put it in code so that it could not be tampered with. But he had forgotten about Lee. . . .

"Rosalie!" Buck bellowed in the direction of the kitchen. "Bring in steak an' eggs for our guest!"

Luke sat down in a chair facing Buck. Lee didn't look at him. The man seemed far away, lost in some bitter backwash of memory. Mel eyed Riatt with unconcealed hate. Except for his father's restraining injunction, Luke knew, this man would have killed him before this.

Rosalie came in from the kitchen. She was dressed in a peasant blouse and tight Levi's which accentuated the roundness of her hips.

She came to the table, carrying Luke's breakfast. She didn't look at anyone. She put the plate down in front of Luke, and the big Ranger saw the discolored bruises on her face. She kept her eyes on the floor as she turned and walked back to the kitchen.

"Heard a lot about you, Riatt," Buck said affably. "Even if I believed only half what I heard, it'd make you about nine feet tall. Reg'lar caterwampus. Tougher'n a bull buff'ler an' twice as smart as the next man. Fastest man with a Colt in Texas—there's a lot of men who think yo're the fastest man in the country. Might be," he mused thinly. "Might be."

Luke picked at his food. His mouth was cut, and eating hurt. But he kept on eating, letting Buck talk. The man was leading up to something.

Buck seemed mighty pleased with himself—pleased enough to show Riatt this much hospitality.

"Lee said you'd come after him," the boss of Broken Crown continued. "I didn't believe it. Told him no Ranger would be that kind of a darn fool. But," he shrugged, "turned out Lee was right. An' it turned out fine—for me!"

He took the cheroot from his mouth and drained his coffee mug. There was a half-filled whiskey bottle in front of him, and he poured a generous slug into the mug and thinned it with bitter black brew from the pot at his elbow.

"The Cordero boys like it fine, too."

Luke kept his silence, his face grim.

"You been givin' him an' his men a lot of grief." Buck grinned. "They want you more than they want guns now. An' I'm gonna give you to them, Riatt!"

The big Ranger sipped his coffee. He knew Buck had been baiting him—he knew that the Broken Crown boss was aware that he and Lee had taken Malino in, that Luke had turned Malino over to the authorities of Ysleta and that Malino would very likely hang.

And he knew the Cordero brothers and how they worked. They would kill Riatt with a cruelty that would make the Stringers look like amateurs.

Buck was puffing contentedly on his cigar. "I've been wanting a free hand along this strip of Border for years, Ranger. Yo're gonna give it to me—you an' the Corderos!"

Luke's gaze held bleak anger. "You've been left alone up here, Buck. Don't push your luck too far!"

Buck chuckled. "Who's gonna stop me, Riatt? The Rangers? When I get through there won't be any organization left in Texas known as the Texas Rangers!"

Luke's grin was contemptuous. "That's big talk, Buck."

Buck reached out and prodded Smith. "Read Mr. Riatt's letter to Captain Hughes, Sawbones."

Smith looked up from the note he was writing. He fixed his spectacles firmly on the bridge of his nose, coughed gently, and began to read:

"Dear Captain Hughes:

Ran into something up here in the Tombstones that has made me forget Lee Stringer for the time being. The Broken Crown bunch is teaming with the Corderos for a raid across the Rio Grande. They're going to hit the towns of Ciba, La Plata and Cody and wipe them out. I have definite proof they will meet in a little canyon just east of Ciba on Thursday, the 10th. They don't know that I know. If you can round up the company and get them by rail to El Paso, you can make it on schedule. I'll be waiting for you at the bend in the river, just below La Plata. This is our big chance to wipe out both Border gangs. I'll be expecting you. Signed: Luke Riatt, Sergeant, Texas Rangers."

The big Ranger listened with a thin smile on his hard lips. "Nice letter," he admitted. "But it won't fool Captain Hughes. It isn't in my writing —and it isn't in code."

Buck laughed. "It'll be in yore handwritin', Riatt." He jerked a thumb toward Smith. "Sawbones ain't much of a cowhand. He can't ride worth a hoot, and he's scairt of guns, an' he still don't know a yearlin' from a goat. But he's the best forger west of the Mississippi. An' with a copy of the letter he got yuh to write for him, he's turned out the neatest bit of handwritin' you'd care to see!" He saw the grim look which spread across Luke's face, and he guffawed. "As to the code part—" He looked at Lee. "Tell him, son!"

Lee didn't raise his eyes from the table. His voice was flat, disinterested. "I'll put it in Ranger code, Paw, like I promised."

Riatt pushed back in his chair, his voice like chilled steel. "You've slid a long way down, Lee—a long way. I hope you burn in Hades a long time for this!"

Mel emptied his mug of coffee into Luke's face. The Ranger came up out of his chair, but

Mel's Colt stopped him. The hump-shouldered killer's voice came harshly, striking across the table.

"Mebbe the Cordero brothers won't get to you first after all, Ranger!"

"Shut up, Mel!" Buck's voice was a harsh bellow from the head of the table. "Eat yore breakfast, Riatt!" he growled as Mel sank back. "The Corderos have first call on you. An' they'll want you healthy. They have their own peculiar ideas of how to break you down."

CHAPTER ELEVEN

A thousand dollars was a powerful inducement to men who were paid thirty a month. And the Idaho Kid, the young, tough, quick-tempered hand who had taken up Mel's rash offer, was determined he'd be the one to bring in the big Ranger's roan and collect the reward.

He knew the country and the few waterholes, and he figured he'd have a noose on the roan within the day. . . . He made two mistakes. He underestimated the roan's cunning, and he didn't count on Red Shale . . . a Broken Crown rider who hated the Idaho Kid.

The Kid first caught sight of the roan when he topped Castle Mesa. The animal, still wearing Riatt's saddle, was moving slowly below him. He looked tired, and the Kid, sensing an easy run-down, shoved his piebald down the slope after him.

The roan broke into an easy run as the Kid came up behind him, and though the Kid pushed the piebald for all he was worth, the roan kept ahead of him.

The Kid gave up finally, not wishing to wind-break his cayuse. He decided then that the only way he'd catch the roan would be to waylay him at the Buckhorn Springs waterhole.

He pulled up in the scant shade of a lone, gnarled wild oak and dismounted, giving his animal a chance to rest while he rolled a brown paper cigaret and smoked it, hunkered down on his heels.

He was twenty-two, a wild, sandy-haired, wiry man with a fair skin that didn't brown easily. He looked boyish from a distance, but a close-up view of the Kid revealed his maturity . . . a hard and bitter stamp of years marked irrevocably by his eyes, by the lines around a dissatisfied mouth.

He had been abandoned as a baby by his parents, brought up among strangers. He had known few kind words in his life, and love was a foreign word with which he had no association.

A man lived in this world and got what he could from it . . . he asked no quarter because he expected none. This was the way the Kid felt; he had known no other way of living.

He stared out past his tired mount to the brown hot expanse of the Basin. . . . He was too much of a loner to be satisfied working long for any man, although Buck Stringer was the kind of boss he understood and grudgingly admired. He had planned to drift on before year's end, with no particular destination in mind. . . . He couldn't go back to Idaho, or Wyoming either, for that matter, without risking a noose. But Mexico was safe, and the unsettled conditions there suited his temperament. . . . A man handy with a gun could get along anywhere in a country like that.

Mel's surprise offer had opened up a new vista for the Kid. A thousand dollars would go a long way in Mexico. . . .

He straightened quickly, heeling out his cigaret as a rider showed up, coming along the wash just south of the oak. He was a lanky, sardonic man, at least ten years older than the Kid; his red hair was thinning under his flat-crowned black hat.

He pulled up as he caught sight of the Kid, then came on slowly, a smile more wary than welcoming on his lips. . . . He paused by the side of the piebald and looked at the animal, then he shook his head.

"Looks like he gave you quite a run, Kid."

The Kid nodded stiffly. He didn't like this man. Red had a slow, patronizing way of speaking that irritated most men and the Kid in particular.

"He can outrun anything on the ranch, except mebbe Buck's sorrel," the Kid said. He eyed Red's gray horse. "You won't catch him on that."

Red shrugged. "Never planned to run him down," he jabbed. "Saw that the minute I laid eyes on him." He turned in the saddle and made an offhand gesture toward the hot country in the distance.

"Only two waterholes he can make tonight:

Buckhorn Springs or Salt Pan." He turned back to face the Kid. "You figgerin' on Buckhorn Springs?"

The Kid hooked his thumb in his cartridge belt above his holstered Remington and stated his position in a blunt, flat voice.

"I'm figgerin' on takin' him back to the spread alone!"

Red leaned forward and rested his forearms on his saddle; he was no match for the Kid with a holster gun and he didn't want to give him even the barest excuse to draw on him.

"We could cover both waterholes tonight, one man at each," he suggested. He made faint gesture with his shoulders. "Five hundred dollars is still a lot of pesos across the Border."

"A thousand is twice as much," the Kid said coldly. His own smile had a cruel, mocking twist. "I like winner take all myself."

Red nodded slightly. He had not really expected that the Kid would take him up on the fifty-fifty split . . . and he had his own ideas as to who would bring the roan back to the ranch.

Crown Basin was big and wild and a body was easily hidden. . . .

"Think Mel will shell out?" he asked blandly. "A thousand dollars is a lot of pocket money."

"He made the offer!" the Kid snapped. "He'll pay." He grinned coldly. "One thing old Buck Stringer won't stand for is a welcher!"

Red nodded. He turned and looked out into the

distance again. "Well, I'm guessin' he'll come into Salt Pan tonight. That's where I'm headed, Kid. . . ."

The Kid kept his thumb hooked into his belt. "Yore guess is as good as mine."

Red hesitated a moment. "Well, good luck, Kid!"

The Idaho Kid eyed him without comment. He was a lot of things, but he was not a hypocrite. Nor did he turn his back on Red or ease his hand away from his holster.

Red smiled faintly as he swung his cayuse away and sent it at a lope toward a distant mesa.

The Idaho Kid moved up by his horse and watched Red until he faded in the distance. Then he swung up into the saddle, slid his Winchester out of the saddle boot and checked it. Satisfied, and alerted, he put his piebald into a walk toward distant Buckhorn Springs. . . .

Riatt's roan was nowhere in sight when he made the Springs. But this didn't bother the Kid. He let his horse drink deep, then led it into a small coulee back of the small springs waterhole and tethered it.

A small grove of willows shaded the south end of the waterhole. He made himself comfortable there, keeping in the shade and out of sight of the approaches to the water. He had once run wild horses with a mustanger and he knew some of the impulses that ruled them. . . . Riatt's roan was far from wild, but it was running warily and it would take the same sort of cunning to trap it.

He had his rope with him, a noose shaken out. He settled back after the sun went down and fought the urge for a smoke.

The shadows came quickly after the pink flush faded from the sky; the wind, flowing back from the hills across the Basin, stirred softly among the willows. A coyote started up in the low hills back of the springs, then paused and slunk off as something disturbed it.

The Kid shifted a little and closed his eyes; it had been a hard day, and sleep crowded him now. He let himself succumb to it, knowing himself. He was a light sleeper, and the first sound of the roan coming in to water would alert him. . . .

The man who had disturbed the coyote was not sleepy. He was alert, tense . . . a wary man who knew he was walking close to death. Red Shale knew the Kid would shoot at the sight of him. He had told the Kid he was headed for Salt Pan, and the young Broken Crown rider would know immediately why he was there.

He had left his horse a quarter of a mile back; it had taken him more than thirty minutes to reach this point above the Springs, crawling most of the way, pausing to study every concealing shadow.

From where he now crouched he could see the

waterhole and the small willow clump . . . he knew the Kid had to be holed up here. It was the logical spot for him to lie in wait for the roan. . . . He strained his eyes, probing the shadows, but could not make out the Kid.

He didn't dare crawl closer. So he lay in wait, rifle cuddled to his cheek . . . waiting for a move from the Kid. The Ranger's roan was less important to him than revenge. . . . He had waited a long time for an opportunity like this, a chance to get even with the Kid without incurring Buck Stringer's wrath.

Not that Buck had any special love for the Idaho Kid; the big, violent Broken Crown boss had little tender sentiment for anyone, including his own family. But Stringer bore down hard on inter-bunkhouse feuds. . . .

So Red waited now, eyeing the shadows past the waterhole. He waited a long time. The moon poked its pale crescent above the ragged horizon, its brilliance shamed by the thousand stars that flamed in the purple-black sky. The breeze blew steadily, was cool against his cheek and welcome after the heat of the day. A coyote came down to water and left, startled by some movement from the Kid, unseen under the willows. . . .

Red was beginning to doubt the roan would come, and was considering his own retreat back to his cayuse when Riatt's animal made his first appearance.

He came up along the rim of the dry wash, a tired, dusty, thirsty animal attracted by the scent of water. To Red Shale, looking down from the low sand hill, he was a dark bulk against the starlit background. The dark robbed him of coloring; he could have been any horse, coming in for water. But the saddle, now slightly askew, marked him.

He paused for a long time, sniffing the air. But the breeze was from behind him and he scented nothing to alarm him.

He came on then, moving slowly toward the water.

Up on the hill Red slid his rifle muzzle out in front of him. He had a clear shot at the roan, but it was not the horse he was after. . . .

Down among the willows the Idaho Kid had snapped awake at the first soft clank of an iron-shod hoof. He reached down for his rope, grasped it and came soundlessly to his feet. The roan was coming slowly down toward the water, but some sixth sense warned him. The animal stopped still, ears swiveling to pick up the sound of what he felt was there in the willows.

The Kid waited, not breathing. He had forty feet of rope, and the roan was still too far. The insect chorus was still around him, but closer to the water they made their incessant nightly sound. The roan turned his head slowly toward the water, thirst overriding his caution. He started down again. . . .

The Kid made his move then. He came out fast, knowing the roan would hear him and whirl around to make his run back that way. He had his noose shaken out as the stud did just that.

He tried to catch neck and forefeet in one wide loop, but managed only to cast the rope around the big roan's neck. He settled back, digging in his heels, knowing he was in for a fight.

The roan hit the end of the noose and kept going, but the Kid kept his feet, his heels digging in furrows. The roan slowed, tried to fight the noose, and it gave the Kid a chance to take a quick dally around a willow sapling. . . .

The roan reared high, trying to shake the noose; then it came down and charged him. The Kid stepped nimbly out of the way, and the roan overran the sapling and was brought up short beyond. He stood trembling, trying to tug the rope free. . . .

The Kid chuckled. "Go ahead; wear yoreself out, feller. By mornin' I'm gonna ride yuh into—" Red's bullet, driving into his back between his shoulder blades, sent him pitching forward against the willow sapling. . . . The rifle shot made a loud clear explosion in the night, sending the roan into a wild, frightened frenzy that ended only in complete exhaustion.

He quieted finally, eyeing Shale as he came slowly down the hill. The lanky man carried his rifle in the crook of his arm. He paused by the

Kid's body and looked down at the still figure.

The Kid lay still, barely breathing. . . . He was numb, with a great burning pain in his chest; he knew that one slight move would bring another bullet through the back of his head. He knew he was dying, and he knew, without having to look up, who had shot him. . . . He had no time left for recriminations or regrets.

Shale turned his attention to the roan. It had turned out to be a good night's work, he thought. . . . He had the Kid and Riatt's roan, and a thousand dollars would take him a long way into Mexico.

His voice was soothing. "Easy, boy . . . no sense in fighting it. I'll get you a drink of water."

He didn't hear the Kid, but a sharp quick tingling at the back of his neck warned him of danger. He turned, only half reacting to the warning, not quite believing it, and took the Kid's .45 slug in the pit of his stomach. It drove him back and slammed him down into a sitting position, the rifle flying from his hands. He sat hunched forward, unable to breathe, staring at the Kid who had just managed to clear his Colt from holster and thrust it out along the ground in front of him.

The Kid's smile had a bloody twist. He shot again and twice more. All the bullets struck Red, but the first shot had been enough.

He keeled over and lay still, and the roan stood

quiet, too, too spent to react more violently than by the nervous quivering of muscles.

The Kid looked at him. He had loved nothing on earth, and it was not love for the roan that made him reach for his belt knife and cut the rope free of the willow. The act was caused rather by a carry-over of hate for Red, and was a last bitter dig at Fate. If he was unable to take the roan in, he didn't want anyone else to have the chance either.

He lay on his face after the effort of cutting the rope and didn't move. The roan pulled back on the rope and it came free. He backed slowly and the rope followed him, slithering over the dark ground across Red's hunched body.

He stopped and shook his head, the bit irons jingling in the stillness. He couldn't understand what had happened, but he knew there was no longer any danger from these two men.

He turned and walked down to the waterhole and drank his fill.

CHAPTER TWELVE

Red Shale's horse drifted into Broken Crown the next day, arousing cynical speculation as to what had happened between him and the Kid. Buck Stringer, hearing of Mel's offer somewhat belatedly, tongue-lashed Mel into sullen anger. Mel was dispatched to fetch the Kid.

He returned at midnight, with the Kid's horse and the two bodies lashed across the piebald's saddle. They were buried the next morning, without ceremony and without markers, in an area overlooking a dry wash.

Buck Stringer gathered his men together and gave strict orders cancelling Mel's offer of a reward for the Ranger's roan. They had more urgent business to attend to; looking grimly at his son, he averred that no horse in Texas was worth a thousand dollars.

Luke Riatt heard the orders from inside the bunkhouse. He had been there for three days now, and he greeted each morning with decreasing hope of success. He was kept padlocked to his bunk during the day and night, except for meals and other necessary functions, and was always escorted or watched by an armed guard.

He came to know something of Broken Crown. It was a big, sprawling, loosely knit place, without pretensions of any sort. Luke got the feeling of an armed camp that could be struck at a moment's notice. He came to believe that a raid in force against the place would have little effect on the outlaw organization. Buck Stringer ran his outlaw bunch from this present headquarters, but he had little camps scattered all over the Tombstones and across the Border in Mexico, and he could retreat to any one of them if necessary.

Captain Hughes had doubtless been aware of this and, knowing it, had let Riatt talk him into letting Luke come into Crown Basin alone. One man might have a chance to take Lee Stringer in, where a company would only send Buck and his men across the Line. . . .

He had muffed his chance. Riatt thought of this through the long hot days and the longer nights. He had walked into a trap because of a woman, and because he had believed in Lee Stringer's fairness. Perhaps he had expected too much. Lee Stringer had been a Ranger once. But he was a Stringer first, and he had killed a man and a woman, even if in his tortured mind he had deemed the killing just. And there was no justification for the money he had stolen from the stage, although Riatt now suspected that Lee's action in taking the money had been more in the nature of defiance than a calculated robbery. He was quite sure no one on Broken Crown knew of the stage robbery or of the money Lee had taken—and Lee gave no inkling as to what he had done with it.

So Luke lay chained to his bunk and brooded on what had happened. He had not foreseen Buck Stringer's tieup with the Corderos, or paid much heed to the rumored threats of Matilde and Ramon against him. The Corderos were among those perennial peasant leaders of Mexico who through oratory and energy rose to shake their fists at the harsh rule of the local government. Often it turned out to be a game of politics by which men like Ramon and Matilde were paid with appointment to some high office, or through outright money bribes, to depart their stated cause. Always it was the ignorant rabble who followed them who suffered.

The Corderos had grown to be a thorn in the side of the Mexican *rurales* as well as of the Texas Rangers. They raided both sides of the Border indiscriminately, somehow always managing to keep just one step out of reach of both Texas lawmen and Mexican militia.

But now the Corderos were going to team up with Buck Stringer. Both camps were bossed by unscrupulous, hard-fisted men—both were outlaws with a tough following. Between them, Luke knew, they could wipe out what little law and order resided in the vast, scantily populated area below Crown Basin.

Luke's hands clenched at his helplessness, and the blond, scarred-cheek man whose name Luke had heard mentioned as Jingo Bob stirred and lifted his eyes from the old magazine he was reading and measured Luke with a cold, hard glance. He stood up and came over, standing far enough away to be out of Riatt's reach, and surveyed the padlocks.

"Rattle 'em, Ranger!" he taunted. "You need the exercise." He turned and walked to his seat and settled back.

Rosalie Stringer came into the bunkhouse with the noon meal on a tin tray covered by a towel to protect the food from the flies. Jingo Bob sat up, his gaze traveling slowly over her trim, well-rounded figure. Up to now it had been Buck Stringer's wife who had brought Luke's food.

Rosalie stopped just inside the bunkhouse; her dull, uncaring glance picked up Luke on his bunk and she walked over to him. The shock of Coley's death and her recapture seemed to have snuffed out whatever spark of rebellion remained in her; she glanced indifferently at Luke, then over at Jingo Bob who came toward them.

Jingo Bob indicated the wooden box by Luke's bunk. "Put it on that," he said.

Rosalie set the tray down. Jingo Bob came up,

lifted the towel from the food . . . tortillas and stew, an odd combination.

He turned to her. "What's happened to yore maw?"

"She asked me to come," Rosalie answered. "She was busy with something else."

Jingo Bob put a hand on her shoulder. "Yo're sure a purty woman, even if you are a half-breed," he muttered. "Mebbe, if you were a little nicer to me, I'd get you out—"

She didn't try to pull away; she looked him in the eye with cold contempt. "Take your hand off me!"

His fingers tightened harshly. "Think I'm not good enough for you, eh? If it wasn't for—"

Luke lunged against his chains, trying to reach him. He knew it was useless, but the sudden motion on his part startled Jingo Bob. He whirled and stepped back, his face whitening before he realized that Luke was helpless; then his face darkened as he became aware of the poor figure he had just cut in front of this girl. He palmed his Colt, intending to batter Luke with it.

Rosalie stopped him. Her voice cut coldly at him. "Pa and Mel have gone. But Lee's in the house! One scream and he'll be here—"

Jingo Bob slowly holstered his Colt. He took a long slow breath. "Rattle them, Ranger," he repeated stiffly. "You ain't got much longer to hang around here."

He started to turn away. Luke raised his right hand. "You forgot something," he said flatly.

Jingo Bob turned, took a key out of his pocket and carefully unlocked Luke's right hand. With this Luke was allowed to eat, picking as best as he could at the food on the tray. . . .

Rosalie looked at Luke. "You tried to help me—and Coley, didn't you?"

Luke shrugged. "I made a poor job of it."

Rosalie's gaze remained on him, searching his face, seeing him for the first time. She smiled sadly. "You tried to help us—and you didn't even know us."

"He came out here to get yore brother," Jingo Bob interrupted harshly, "not to help anybody! He's a Ranger, Rosalie! If he could, he'd see us all hang!"

Rosalie turned, looked at the blond, tough Broken Crown rider. "If I could, I'd do the same," she said quietly. Then she turned and walked out of the bunkhouse back to the ranchhouse.

Luke looked after her thoughtfully, hiding the first faint stirring of hope he'd felt in the three days he'd been chained there. . . .

He didn't see Rosalie again. Tina Stringer, heavy, impassive, brought him his meals again, and Jingo Bob managed to wreak revenge on Luke in small, unobtrusive ways, such as dropping his cigaret butt into Luke's coffee or jamming the muzzle of his Colt hard against Luke's back as Luke bent over the tray to eat. Goaded into bitter fury, Luke lashed back with his free hand, catching Jingo Bob across the mouth and sending him stumbling back. This was all the excuse the man needed . . . he used his gun butt to batter Luke into unconsciousness.

On the morning of the fifth day a slim, scarred Mexican rode into Broken Crown. He sat a fine palomino horse and he rode with proud and regal bearing. His name was Jose Ferrito, and he was the right-hand man of the Cordero brothers.

Luke Riatt sat up as Buck Stringer and the newcomer came into the bunkhouse. Jingo Bob stood up respectfully.

Buck Stringer looked at Luke, then over to Jingo Bob. "He been givin' yuh trouble?"

Jingo Bob shrugged. "I calmed him down some," he said. He stepped back as Jose Ferrito walked slowly between the bunks and paused, putting his dark, level stare on the big Ranger. A growth of wiry black beard darkened Luke's face, hiding the discolored bruises. The puffiness was gone from Luke's cut lips and the soreness from his body. He returned the Mexican's level stare with a cold appraisal.

Ferrito nodded slowly, then turned to Buck. "It looks like him, *Señor* Stringer."

"It *is* him!" Buck growled. "Take my word for it, if that badge ain't enough—"

"A badge like that can be had by anyone who wishes it badly enough," Jose murmured. "It need not be the Ranger Luke Riatt behind it."

"Why should I try to fool you?" Buck snapped impatiently. "Take my word for it: he's Luke Riatt. Matilde and Ramon will know when I bring him to the rendezvous."

Ferrito shrugged. "That is so," he agreed. "And the guns?"

"Two hundred rifles. And five thousand rounds, plus two cases of dynamite. You have my word."

Jose considered this. "We can most surely use the rifles, the dynamite and the rounds," he admitted. "With them we can—" He sighed softly. "But the risk is very great, *Señor* Stringer. To help you raid the Triangle—to plunder the towns you play . . . ?" He raised his shoulders with Latin expressiveness. "It is too great a risk for us. It might cause an international incident—"

"Why should that bother Ramon and Matilde?" Buck sneered. "With the rifles they can force concessions from the Governor of Chihuahua— they can even put themselves in power, if it is what they wish. What will they have to fear from anyone on this side of the Border?"

"The U.S. Army moves slowly, we know," Jose said sharply. "But the Texas Rangers, *señor*—we have met them before."

Stringer put a frowning silence between them. He walked to the near bunk and picked up a Winchester carbine stacked against the wall. He turned and tossed it to Jose, who caught it expertly and wonderingly.

"Two hundred rifles like this one, an' my promise that Luke Riatt will be theirs, to do with as they wish." He paused, a sneer on his broad face. "An' to make sure that the great Corderos will have nothing more to fear, I promise them that the backbone of the Texas Rangers will be smashed *before* we plunder the Triangle!"

Jose frowned. "The rifles I believe. Riatt I see before me. But this other—" He shook his head.

Buck Stringer pointed a gnarled finger at the big Ranger. "You know of this man, Jose. He is one of Ranger Captain Hughes' most trusted lieutenants. He is the man who has given you so much trouble . . . he is the man who is gonna be our bait." He smiled as Jose stared at him. "Bait for a trap into which Captain Hughes will lead the flower of the Texas Rangers!"

Jose licked his lips in greedy anticipation. "It is a bold undertaking," he agreed, "if it can be done!"

"It will be done!" Buck snapped. "Southeast of the town of Ciba lies the canyon of the Placerita. Company D will have to ride through it to the rendezvous I have arranged for them; a rendezvous they believe planned by Luke Riatt."

111

Jose frowned. "You have managed this?" he asked doubtfully.

Buck nodded. "You forget that my son Lee rode with the Rangers, Jose . . . he learned their ways well." As Jose's lips twisted cynically: "By this time Captain Hughes will have received a letter in Riatt's own handwriting, and in Ranger code. They will come without question, Jose—and they will ride into the muzzles of our guns. Think of it—together we will smash forever the might of the Texas Rangers!"

A flicker of admiration at the boldness of the scheme streaked Jose's sabre-scarred face. "It is possible, *señor.*" He looked at Riatt. "The rifles we need. But for this man—ah, for this man, Ramon and Matilde will agree to your terms, *Señor* Stringer."

Buck grinned. "Then tell them I'll meet them at Pico Canyon. I'll have the rifles and the ammunition with me. And I'll have Luke Riatt!"

They went out together, leaving the Ranger chained to his bunk. By the wall Jingo Bob rolled a toothpick between his teeth and grinned.

CHAPTER THIRTEEN

That night Lee Stringer came to the bunkhouse. He stood in the doorway, watching Luke. He seemed aged—his eyes had a dark, tortured appeal in them.

Luke was watching Jingo Bob play solitaire. The rider had shucked his gunbelt and left it hooked on a nail above him. He looked up as Lee approached, glanced quickly to his gunbelt. He didn't trust Lee Stringer, but he was the boss' son.

Lee made a motion with his thumb. "Wait outside," he told Bob.

Jingo hesitated. He had his orders, but they did not extend to Buck Stringer's boys. He shrugged, tossed his deck on his bunk and swaggered out-side.

Lee sat on the edge of the bunk facing Riatt. He was silent, choosing his words. "Luke," he said slowly, "I didn't mean to kill her. I want you to believe that. I didn't want to kill her." He shuffled his feet and looked down at his hands. "It was an accident—a terrible mistake."

Luke eyed the man with a cold, unflattering regard. Lee was a far different man from the cocky, arrogant Ranger he had known.

"What about the driver?" he asked quietly. "Was shooting him an accident, too?"

"It was me or him," Lee said. "I didn't shoot to kill him."

"Maybe that will rate you a good word in Purgatory," Luke said dryly. "But I'm not forgetting that there was twenty thousand dollars in the strongbox—"

"I don't know why I took it," Lee countered. His eyes held a desperate appeal for understanding. "I didn't need the money. Never intended to keep it." His voice lowered. "No one here knows about it. I've buried the money in back of Shawlee's barn, at the foot of the pepper tree. Even Pete Shawlee doesn't know about it."

Riatt studied the ex-Ranger with sudden hope. His glance went to the gunbelt over Jingo Bob's bunk. His own gunbelt was rolled up on top of Jingo Bob's foot locker under the bunk. Both guns were less than twenty feet away, but they might as well have been twenty thousand miles off. . . .

"Lee," he said coldly, "I can't promise you anything. But get me out of here and I'll see that you get a fair trial. Help me get away from here before Captain Hughes and Company D ride into the trap you helped your father set. Do this and maybe I'll—"

Mel's loud voice, snarling at Jingo Bob outside,

interrupted them. Lee got to his feet. His voice was low. "I'm not leaving here, Luke. I decided that when I rode away from Chuckawalla Wells. I'm never going to leave Broken Crown."

He turned as Mel strode into the bunkhouse, his glance measuring Riatt and his brother with quick suspicion. "Paw's lookin' for yuh," he growled at Lee. "We got a powwow comin' up. You better be there!"

Lee shrugged. He turned and walked out. Mel levelled a sneering glance at Riatt before following his brother.

Vince Stringer stirred as Lee and Mel came into the room. He reached for his cup of bitter black coffee liberally spiked with raw whiskey. He was sitting at one end of the long table, facing Buck . . . behind him the shades were drawn against the day's heat.

This was a Stringer powwow, and no one else was included. . . .

Buck waited as Mel slid into a chair. Lee remained standing by the door.

"Yo're in on this," Buck growled, waving Lee to a chair. He watched Lee settle into the chair opposite Mel, then turned to Vince whose arm was still in a sling.

"You were sayin'?" he asked harshly.

Vince shrugged. "I've known the Cordero boys as long as you," he said bluntly. "I've never trusted them further than the end of a gun muzzle." He shook his head slowly. "Give them two hundred rifles an' they'll run us out of the Triangle, too!"

Buck looked from his brother to Mel and Lee. His lips had a tight, self-satisfied crimp. "Yo're gettin' old, Vince," he growled. "They'll get two hundred rifles, like I promised, an' ammunition, like I said. But—" his face split into a wide grin—"the ammunition won't fit the rifles. An' carbines without firing pins are useless, Vince."

Vince stiffened. "Matilde an' Ramon ain't fools. They'll check—"

"Not before we wipe out Ranger Company D," Buck snapped.

Vince took a deep breath. "And then—?"

Buck put his gaze on Mel. "We have plans for the Corderos, Mel an' I. An'—" he turned to Lee—"you, too, son. You're ridin' with us!"

Lee shook his head. "I told you no. I'm staying here."

Mel sneered: "Let him stay, Paw! He won't be any use to us—"

"Shut up!" Buck snarled. He leaped forward across the table. "I've waited three weeks for you to snap out of it, son; let you lie around, doin' nothin'—feelin' sorry for yoreself. Now there's work to be done."

"I've done what you wanted of me!" Lee interrupted harshly. "What more do you want?"

"I want you to be there when we smash those Rangers," Buck said grimly.

Lee shook his head. "You don't need me."

Buck stared at him. "You fool! They'd hang you if they got hold of you. You know that?"

Lee shrugged.

Vince said quietly: "Let him be, Buck. He's done enough for you, sendin' out that letter."

Buck eyed Lee with sudden grim suspicion. "I don't know," he said slowly. "I don't know what he wrote in that letter—"

Vince cut in sharply. "He wrote what you told him." He turned to Lee. "Didn't you?"

Lee was looking at his father, studying him. He had never been afraid of this broad, powerful, violent man since he had been old enough to stand up to him, but like his brother Mel and the others on the ranch, he had taken Buck's orders. It was a wild, rough spread, remote from even the Border towns, and Buck had been the law out there—the giver and taker of favors. Lee had known little else until he had left Broken Crown and met Milly and married her. But he had learned there was more to life than Broken Crown when he had joined the Texas Rangers.

Now he shook his head slowly, not answering his uncle but speaking directly to his father, shifting to a topic which had been bothering him.

"You've got a hundred square miles in which to range Broken Crown beef, Paw . . . you don't

117

need the Triangle an' the grief it'll bring you. And you don't need the Cordero brothers. . . ."

Buck sneered at him. "A hundred square miles of sand and rock. . . ." He shook his head. "Son, I want more than that. An' the Triangle is only the beginnin'. When I get through the Stringers will be runnin' all of West Texas!"

Lee settled back slowly, knowing it was useless to argue.

Vince was frowning, remembering that Lee had not answered his question. He eyed the ex-Ranger uneasily.

Lee said slowly: "You don't need me, Paw. Mel's right. I'd only be in the way—"

Buck stood up slowly and pointed a gnarled finger at Lee. "I don't give a hang if you just sit there an' let the Rangers take pot shots at you when we ambush them in Placerita Canyon. But I promised I'd have every man Jack on the spread out there—an' that includes you!"

He turned abruptly to Mel and made a curt gesture to the door. "Get the boys ready—we're pickin' up the rifles now. Hitch up the two hide wagons and throw in grub for a couple of days—"

He waited until Mel had gone, then looked back to Lee. "I'll be back in two days. You be ready to ride or, by thunder, I'll take the whip to you!"

Lee looked at Vince, then back to his father; he nodded with a bitter smile. "All right, Paw . . . I'll ride with you. Just one thing . . . for me."

Buck scowled. "What?"

"Let Riatt go."

Buck stared at him.

Lee stood up, facing him. "The day we ride to Placerita Canyon, turn him loose, afoot. He won't be able to warn Captain Hughes . . . it'll be all over before he can even reach the nearest town." He paused, took a slow breath. "I rode with him, Paw. Never even got to like him. But I got to respect him and what he stood for—"

Buck's voice was flat, even. "He came to hang you!"

Lee shrugged. "He came because it was his job . . . and I knew he'd be coming. He came to bring me back to stand trial for killing Milly."

"She deserved killing!" Buck said harshly.

"No. She deserved better than I gave her . . . maybe even better than Mason could give her. She sure deserved better than this." Lee made a quick, savage gesture toward the kitchen.

"All she was here was a galley slave . . . someone to cook and wash and mend, like Maw and Rosalie. She was a woman when I met her —only a waitress in a cheap lunchroom, but a woman. She smiled a lot." Lee paused, looking back on the years. His voice was softly bitter. "She even laughed. But she quit laughin' up here, like Rosalie an' Maw. She was here six months and she looked ten years older—"

Buck cut in harshly: "She wasn't worth the

food we fed her. I told you what she was the day you brought her home!"

"I'll always hate myself," Lee said quietly, "for believing you!"

Buck looked at him for a moment, then turned to Vince. "I'll keep Jingo Bob in the bunkhouse with Riatt, an' I'll send Mel back before the wagons. I want Luke Riatt to be here when I get back. I want him here even if you have to kill Lee to stop him!"

Vince nodded slowly, his eyes on Lee. "Riatt'll be here," he promised.

Buck went out, slamming the door behind him. In the sudden silence the sounds of men saddling, hitching the wagons, drifted into the room. . . .

Vince said softly: "You never answered me, Lee."

Lee looked at him, frowning.

"You did write what yore father told you," Vince persisted.

Lee looked at him coldly. "I wrote what he wanted," he said shortly. He turned away then and went into the kitchen, and Vince looked after him, his doubts mounting. If Lee had lied to Buck, they'd all be riding into a trap. . . .

He stood up then and turned to the door. But when he got out to the porch, Buck and the others were already gone. He could see them in the distance, heading for North Pass.

He slouched against the rickety porch support and rolled himself a cigaret with his good

120

hand. . . . It would be time enough to press this with Lee when Buck and the boys rode back. . . .

Lee paused in the kitchen to look at the woman who was his stepmother . . . a woman who had raised him, to whom he had gone for comfort and for peace during the trials of his boyhood. An impassive, silent woman who had never complained at her lot, who had performed the heavy, endless work of looking after and cooking for the Stringers . . . an unobtrusive tireless mechanism who kept the housekeeping going at the sprawling spread.

She used to run a hand through his hair when he cried, her gentle, stubby fingers speaking for her, soothing more than words could have. . . . She had sat by his bedside through measles and mumps, like some big, gentle, watchful dog. She loved him, he knew, but she never spoke of it. . . . She was the same to him and Mel as she was to Rosalie, of her own flesh and blood. She was making corn tortillas, rolling them out on the big round stone by the sink, her hands turning and slapping the rolled dough with the quick dexterity of a lifetime. Her Mexican-Indian blood showed in the dark flush of her cheeks. The stone she had brought with her when, as a young comely girl, she had come to live there at Broken Crown. She cooked mainly what Buck Stringer wanted, which was mostly tough beef or hash; the tortillas were her addition, a link with her past, and Lee had often watched her at the little ceremony of their making.

She sensed his presence and turned her head to look at him; there was neither smile nor word between them, but the warmth was still there, in her eyes, and he felt a heavy sadness now at all the heedless times when he had ignored her. He walked up to her and put a hand against her cheek; she looked startled, and he withdrew it, smiled a little and walked out through the back door, into the heat and sunlight of the afternoon.

Rosalie was at the big copper tub under the gnarled oak tree, poling dirty clothes in the steaming water. . . . She paused to brush hair from her face, unaware of Lee's presence. He watched her for a moment, sharply aware now of all the little things he had never noticed before . . . feeling like a man who knows he will not ever be seeing those things again, and regretting the lost years. . . .

Rosalie bent to the heavy oaken bucket, and he walked quickly to her, taking it from her hands and emptying it into the big copper tub for her.

She flashed him a small quick smile and picked up the pole and stirred the mass of soiled, dirty clothes, turning and twisting them in the hot, soapy water. . . . There was sweat on her face, making it shiny . . . it was the way Milly's face had shone. Only hers had been rebellious, pouting. . . .

"Rosalie," he said softly, "get away from here. Go somewhere, a long way from Broken Crown."

She froze on the pole, looking at him, startled. . . . He had always been kinder to her than Mel, but there had been little familiarity between them even after he had brought Milly back with him.

"Go away?" She took a slow, sad breath. "I tried that."

"With Coley," he said quickly. "That was a mistake."

"He was a nice boy," she defended him.

"That's all he was," Lee said: "a boy. He didn't belong here on Broken Crown." He took her arm, his voice low, intense.

"It took me a long time to find out there's other ways of living. . . . I don't want you to make the same mistake." He turned his head, shooting a quick glance to the bunkhouse where Riatt was being kept a prisoner.

"Luke's a man, Rosalie. When he goes, go with him!"

Rosalie stared at him. "Go where?" She shook her head. "Pa'll never let him go. He's going to take the Ranger with him."

"No! He'll be gone before Paw gets back." His fingers tightened on her arm. "Remember, when Luke goes—go with him!"

He turned away before she could answer and walked back into the house.

CHAPTER FOURTEEN

Mel Stringer rode into the hot, dusty yard at noon the next day. He came in leading Riatt's roan at the end of the Idaho Kid's rope, still looped around his neck. Mel had left Buck and the others at North Pass to check the sentry shack above the Basin gap; circling back toward the ranch, he had come upon the roan, the trailing rope tangled around a mesquite bush.

He came within a hair trigger's breadth of killing the animal there; then he remembered Riatt, and the pummeling he had received at the big Ranger's fists, and characteristically he decided to take out his vengeance on both man and animal.

Broken Crown was practically deserted as he pulled up by the corral and tied the roan to a corral post. Vince and Lee were in the ranch-house. Jingo Bob was inside the bunkhouse with Riatt. The women were nowhere in sight.

Riatt was lying down on his bunk when he heard Mel come back. It had been unusually quiet all morning, and the midday heat had put Jingo Bob to sleep over the old newspaper he had been reading.

The ring of shod hoofs on the sun-baked ground

roused him. He threw his paper aside and got up, stretching. He was getting bored with his job.

Luke's voice came through the close heat of the bunkhouse. "I thought Jingo Bob rated a more important job than nursemaid. Seems I heard the name rated pretty high on Cochise County wanted posters."

Luke wanted to get under Jingo Bob's skin, but the man only gave Luke a bleak, level look and walked to the door.

Luke watched him shape up a cigaret. He could see the patch of ground beyond Bob, and he wondered who had returned to Broken Crown. And then he heard a horse's high shrill scream and he grew tense on the bunk, a knot tightening in the pit of his stomach.

Jingo Bob stepped aside as Mel Stringer filled the doorway. Mel's face was dark and sweaty and his shirt showed big patches of sweat. He looked at Riatt, and a dark streak of triumph glinted in his eyes.

"I got a surprise for yuh, Ranger! A real surprise!" He turned to Jingo. "Unlock him. Get him outside. I want him to see this."

He turned and stamped out, and Jingo Bob came slowly between the bunks to where Luke lay. He unlocked the Ranger and stepped back, the heel of his right hand on his Colt butt. He nodded coldly. "You heard Mel. Get up an' walk outside . . . slow an' easy."

Luke rubbed his hands together. He swung his legs over the side and stood up and walked to the door, pausing in the bright harsh sunlight, squinting his eyes against the glare.

His roan was tied to the corral post between the bunkhouse and the sprawling ranchhouse. Blankets and saddle had been stripped from him; his saddle was dumped by the wooden horse trough. The roan was fighting the rope which held him to the corral post.

Luke put his back against the bunkhouse wall, five feet from the door. Rosalie Stringer, he saw, was just coming up from the spring behind the ranchhouse. She was carrying a bucket of water, and it was the first time Luke had seen her since the day she had brought him his noon day meal.

She looked at Luke and at Jingo Bob who was standing in the doorway. She put the water bucket down and stumbled, and water spilled out onto the dry, dusty ground. There was no display of temper. She picked up the bucket and turned back to the spring. . . .

Mel Stringer had disappeared inside the ranchhouse. He came out now, holding a lead-tipped quirt. Vince Stringer came out to the veranda and settled in the big, rawhide-backed chair, his arm still in a sling. He was puffing on a corncob pipe.

Mel started to walk toward Riatt's roan. "Ran him down myself, Ranger," he said. His voice rang harshly across the hot yard; it held incalculable cruelty. "He was tangled up in a mesquite bush, draggin' the Idaho Kid's rope."

The big roan turned to eye the hump-shouldered man with the quirt. His sleek-muscled body quivered, and he whistled angrily.

"I'm gonna cut him to ribbons, Ranger!" Mel snarled. "When I get through with him there won't be enough hide left to cover the palm of yore hand!"

The quirt cut through the air and left its mark across the roan's flank. The big stud lunged and fought the rope, and Mel chuckled, an ugly sound, underlining the roan's angry whistling.

The Ranger's hands clenched, and he took a step forward. Jingo Bob's voice held him. "Easy, Ranger!"

Mel's thick arm swung again. Sweat ran down his dark, stubbled cheeks. He backed away as the roan wheeled and kicked out at him, and his laughter rang out in the hot afternoon.

"Mel!" Lee's voice crackled sharply in the momentary quiet. "Mel! Don't hit him again!"

Mel's arm was pulled back, his shoulder muscles bunched under his shirt. He turned his head. Lee had come out to the porch; he was standing slack against the porch support by the steps. His belt gun was strapped to his hip.

Mel's face darkened. "Keep out of this!" he snarled.

"Don't use that quirt again!" Lee warned. His voice was tight. "I've had enough of your stinking brutality! Taking it out on a helpless animal is about your size. Leave that horse alone!"

"Wal, darn yore righteous hide!" Mel sneered. He dropped the quirt and turned around, facing his brother like some lobo backed into a coulee. His voice rasped in the bright afternoon. "You warnin' me?"

Vince Stringer came to his feet. "Lee!" he growled. "Mel! Use yore heads! What's a hoss to you?"

Lee ignored his uncle. He was eyeing Mel, his face tense. "Cut that stud loose, Mel!"

The hump-shouldered man stared at him. The silence between them was ugly and meaningful. Then Mel shrugged. He started to turn around, took a step toward the corral post. It was enough to ease Lee, put him off guard. Then Mel whirled and fired!

He pumped two shots into his brother and stood spraddle-legged, his dark face twisted, watching Lee fold slowly and fall on his face in the dust at the foot of the steps.

Vince Stringer came to the head of the stairs and looked down at Lee's body. He was holding his pipe tightly, a sick look in his eyes; he raised his gaze to Mel, who stared back at him with cold defiance.

"He drew on me, Vince! You saw him!"

Vince said nothing. He turned and walked back into the house, slamming the door behind him.

Mel sneered. He picked up the quirt he had dropped and turned to face the roan again.

Luke's body was tight, ready for a break. Jingo Bob had stepped down from the door; he was standing slack-hipped a dozen feet from Riatt, watching Mel. He seemed momentarily unaware of Riatt, but Luke knew that the kid would get him before he got around the corner of the bunkhouse if he made a break for it in that direction.

Rosalie's soft voice hit him with gentle shock, like the splashing of cool water. He came up on his toes, turning slightly to look back into the comparative darkness of the bunkhouse.

"It's loaded," Rosalie said quietly. She was just within the doorway, holding Luke's Colt in her hands. As Luke put his startled gaze on her, she tossed his gun to him.

Riatt didn't have time to wonder what had prompted Buck Stringer's daughter to act. He saw Jingo Bob glance at him with sudden alertness. Riatt whirled, feeling the comforting weight of the .45-caliber gun against his palm— he saw Jingo Bob's eyes widen in the split-second before he jerked his muzzle up.

Luke killed him with his first shot.

Mel spun around at the sound. He saw Luke with a smoking gun in his fist and he reacted with the reflexes of a trained killer—he drew and cut down on the Ranger.

Riatt's slugs spun him around, hammering him

with giant blows. He staggered back, fighting to keep his feet, his shots going wild. Then his boots seemed to tangle; he sat down heavily. His head dropped wearily on his chest and he fell sideways.

Luke wasted no movements. Vince Stringer was inside the house. He'd be coming out to see what had happened. Luke made a run for the ranch-house and was at the foot of the stairs when Vince pushed through the screen door.

He jerked up short, staring into the muzzle of the big Ranger's Colt.

Riatt said sharply: "Come down here! Walk over to the bunkhouse. Put your face against the wall and stay like that!"

Vince gave him no argument. He walked past Rosalie, standing in the doorway; he faced the wall with quiet resignation.

Luke glanced down at Lee as he turned away. There was a shocked look still stamped on Lee's face, as though he had not quite been prepared for dying. . . .

Luke pushed a faint regret from his thoughts. Fate had its own way of meting justice, he reflected, and there was a touch of pity in his tone as he murmured, "So long, Lee. . . ."

The roan muzzled him with warm affection as he patted the animal's neck. "We got a ride ahead of us, fella," Luke said. "Think you can hold out?"

The roan whinnied softly.

The Ranger saddled the roan and led him to where the girl was watching. Vince kept his face turned to the bunkhouse wall—he seemed old and stooped and without fight.

Rosalie said brokenly: "Let me ride with you, Ranger. I've got to get away from here. Take me with you!"

Luke hesitated. He owed this girl his life; taking her away from Broken Crown was the least he could do for her.

He heard the screen door open and close softly and he whirled quickly, gun in hand. Tina Stringer had come out to the sagging veranda. She was looking down at Lee's sprawled body with resigned patience.

Luke handed Rosalie his Colt. He indicated Vince. "Don't let him move. I'll be right out."

She took the gun and nodded, her face coming alive with a long-suppressed hatred of the man. Vince Stringer shrank away from her as she faced him.

Luke ran into the bunkhouse, reached under Jingo Bob's bunk and took his gunbelt from the top of Jingo's foot locker. Holding it in his hand, he ran out, not entirely sure of this girl. He saw that she was standing in the sun, holding his Colt with both hands, the hammer cocked back. . . .

"I should kill you," she was saying intensely, "for all the things you've done to me."

Luke strapped his gunbelt about his lean waist.

"Let him be," he said quietly, reaching over her shoulder and taking his gun from her. He eased the hammer down and reloaded the gun and slipped it into his holster. He checked his cartridge belt, finding the loops filled.

"Saddle yourself a mount," he told the girl. "I'll wait for you."

She needed no urging. It took her five minutes to pick out a rangy piebald and saddle it. She rode up beside Luke, a small, slim figure.

Luke stepped up into the roan's saddle. Rosalie pointed to the north where a dust banner marred the sky. Her features were tight, afraid.

"We must hurry," she whispered intensely, "before they get back."

Luke nodded. "Anything you want to take with you?" His voice softened. "I don't expect you'll be coming back."

Rosalie shook her head. She was dressed in a cotton shirt and blue Levi's, and a yellow silk bandanna held her hair in place. "No," she whispered again. "I don't ever want to come back here."

Vince Stringer turned slowly to face them. "You'll never make it, Riatt," he muttered.

"There's only two ways for a hoss out of Crown Basin. An' Buck an' the boys are comin' up out of North Pass now!"

Luke's grin was bleak. "We'll see." He backed the roan away from the bunkhouse and made a motion to the girl. "We'll ride south."

Rosalie nodded, then turned to the house as her mother said: "Rosa," in a dull, flat voice. It was her way of addressing her when she was displeased or angered. It held the girl in the saddle.

Tina Stringer walked ponderously down the steps, bent over Lee's body and picked up the unfired gun he still held in his clenched right hand. She lifted it and cocked it, clumsily but determinedly.

"Rosa! You stay here!"

Rosalie looked at her mother; her face was white with fear. "Mamma," she said, "Mamma, I must go. I can't stay now. . . . I don't want to stay." Her voice sharp, almost breaking. "Mamma, I don't want to live like you have . . . yelled at, kicked at . . . treated worse than those horses in the corral. I—"

Tina Stringer's stolid, uncompromising voice cut through her words, through the hot dry stillness of the yard. "Rosa—you stay!"

Rosalie started to back the piebald away. "No, Mamma—"

The gun kicked heavily in Tina's hands. The piebald staggered and shrilled in pain—it whirled and lunged away, beating a hard tattoo on the sun-baked earth. Rosalie hung on, clutching the piebald's mane.

Luke's Colt was in his fist, aimed at Tina. He didn't want to shoot, but he wasn't going to be shot at. He started to back his roan around, but

Tina was staring with unseeing eyes across the shimmering distance. Smoke leaked from the muzzle of the gun in her hands.

Riatt whirled the big roan around and put him into a hard run after Rosalie's piebald. . . .

Vince Stringer came at a run across the yard toward Tina. "Blast you!" he snarled at the woman. "You had a chance to stop him—and you let him get away!"

Years of browbeating, of smothered hatred, of accepted brutality finally created a reaction in this stolid, impassive woman. She turned to face the man. In the harsh beat of the sun the sprawled figures of her two stepsons seemed unreal. *Blast you!* The curse rang in her ears—she had heard it hurled at her countless times. The muzzle of Lee's Colt lifted, and Vince stopped short a few paces away, his face whitening at what he saw in her face.

"You fool!" he managed to choke out. "Buck'll kill you for—"

The blast lifted him up on his toes. His eyes opened wide with shock as he twisted and fell.

The woman sat down, slowly, deliberately, on the bottom step. She turned her gaze toward North Pass, to the distant riders and the two wagons trailing behind. Buck Stringer was coming home!

She put the muzzle of the gun against her breast and pulled the trigger. . . .

Vince was still alive when Buck and the Broken Crown riders came into the yard. The boss of Broken Crown sat stiffly in the saddle, surveying the carnage. His men bunched around him, staring with shocked wonder at the scene.

Vince had managed to drag himself into the scant shade of the porch. He called out as Buck reined in and his brother swung out of saddle and strode to him, his face an iron, grim mask.

He told Buck what had happened—and he died while telling it.

Buck Stringer glanced toward the far trace of dust marking Luke Riatt's and his daughter's line of flight. He had to stop the big Ranger before he broke out of Crown Basin and warned Captain Hughes and Company D, already on their way to their rendezvous in Placerita Canyon.

He didn't think of his daughter. He'd deal with her when he caught up with her!

"Get fresh hosses, all of you!" he ordered harshly. "He's headed for South Pass. Apache Joe'll hold him until we catch up!"

As his men dismounted and headed for the corrals, he paused a moment to look down at his wife—at his sons. Nothing showed in his face—he was not a man to show emotion. Nor did the loss of this stolid, heavy woman disturb him. For his sons he felt a fleeting regret. Then he turned and followed his men into the corral. . . .

CHAPTER FIFTEEN

South of Broken Crown the land sloped toward Mexico. Broken Crown came in a curve from the north, shouldering the Basin, a wall of crumbly rock rising high above the brush-dotted slopes.

Rosalie's piebald began to falter before it ran the first mile out of Stringer's ranch yard. Riding alongside, Riatt saw blood spurting from the bullet hole just below the right shoulder and knew the piebald wouldn't last another mile.

He looked back over his shoulder. Buck and his riders were coming into Broken Crown from the north, their dust flattening against the distant buildings of the ranch. They'd be riding trail-weary horses, and Luke knew they would have to change mounts before taking up pursuit.

His roan was running with an easy stride and the Ranger knew that without the added burden of Rosalie, the big stallion would have little trouble keeping ahead of most of the men who would soon be on their trail. But he couldn't leave this girl behind—Luke had no illusions as to what would happen to her when Buck Stringer caught up with his daughter.

The piebald's stride broke; he slackened off

to a stumbling walk. His head sagged and his breathing came in a ragged wheezing.

The girl cast a frightened look at Luke.

Riatt rode his roan alongside the dying animal and reached out for the girl just as the piebald shivered violently. Luke lifted her out of saddle and set her down in front of him; the piebald slacked away from Riatt's roan, stumbled and went down, rolling heavily on its side.

Rosalie clung to the big Ranger. He muttered gently: "We'll make it, girl," but he wasn't so sure. The big roan had amazing endurance, but eventually the girl's added one hundred and eight pounds would tell.

Rosalie Stringer buried her face in Luke's shirt, reaction making her shiver. She was leaving behind the only home she knew. And though Broken Crown had been rough and cruel, it had been home.

Lee was dead. He alone of her family had been kind to her, although there had never been any closeness between them. He had lived in his own private world, and now he was dead— killed by Mel. She shuddered and a little moan escaped her. *Mel!* She thought of her hulking half-brother, of the cruel tricks he had played on her, even as a little girl. He had loved to make her scream, to hide her face from him.

Buck Stringer had ignored her. She meant as little to him as her rag doll—he had tolerated her and punished her when she got in his way. She had early learned to shun the big, grim figure who had sired her.

Her mother, an inarticulate woman, she loved and despised. She loved her for the little kindnesses she had shown Rosalie—despised her for her humble submission to her intolerable life. Tina Stringer had been as stolid and emotionless as a machine. She had cooked and washed for Broken Crown, and when Rosalie had grown old enough to help she had been forced into the same harsh bondage.

Only Milly, Lee's wife, had brought a touch of softness, of seeming gentleness, into that land of harsh men. She had lasted six months and then run off with a gambling man she met in Shawlee's Store.

Lee had followed her, and Broken Crown had become a harsh place again, until Coley Prindle had drifted in.

He had been different from the others. He was young and sensitive and dreamy; and he kept himself clean. He was wanted for murder in Missouri, but he didn't look like a killer. She really knew very little about him, except that he had not teased her or tried to make ungentlemanly proposals to her.

Coley had been kind and polite and eventually she had warmed to him. She had been ready, at the time, to warm to any man who showed her any kindness. She had clung to him after that, asking to be taken out of Crown Basin . . . and Coley had agreed. He had been frightened, knowing the sort of man Buck Stringer was, and yet he was touched by her need. And he had been soft enough to plan the flight from Broken Crown.

She did not know how Buck had found out. Her mind still shrank from the memory of what had happened. She had fled from Shawlee's on Riatt's roan and had met Coley just as he was entering North Pass. They had turned back and tried to circle south, hoping to elude the men on the rim. But they had not reckoned with Mel, or with Coley's gray horse which had given out.

When he was forced to rest, Mel had come upon them with his silent Indian tread. Coley had been shot before he could get his gun free. He was not yet dead when Mel had cut his throat, forcing her head up to see, and laughing in that ugly, insane way of his.

All this she told Luke, as he held her, letting the big roan rest. It came out of her between low sobs. She felt small and lost, frightened by what she had left behind and needing an anchor to cling to.

Luke let her talk, keeping his eye on the distant ranch. It would be some time before anyone would be coming after them, and the more the roan rested the better chance they would have of outrunning their pursuers.

She stopped finally, and he heard her sigh; she raised her face to his and smiled a small, searching smile.

"Lee told me to leave with you," she said. "He said you were a good man."

Luke frowned. "Lee told you that?"

She nodded. "He sent me to bring you your gun. I think he knew what Mel was up to when he rode in with your horse. He didn't want his father to bring you to the Corderos. . . ."

She was speaking disjointedly, out of her deep misery, but Luke knew what she was trying to say. Lee had gone through purgatory since that day in Chuckawalla Wells.

"We rode together for almost a year," he told her, "but I never really got to know your brother." He shrugged. "I think it was my fault as much as his." He looked out over her head to the heat haze shimmering, on the flats.

"Lee was the gentlest man on the ranch, outside of Coley," she whispered. "He hated to see me there. He told me I'd soon grow old and fat and—" Her voice broke, and Luke ran his palm over her hair.

"You won't have to go back, Rosalie. I'll see to that."

Her arms tightened about him. "I have no other place to go," she whispered.

"It's a big world beyond Broken Crown," he said quietly. "You'll find a place to settle, once we get out of here."

She looked up at him. "And you—?"

"I'll see a lot of you," he said simply. Then he turned his gaze to the distant ranch, attracted by the small dots of riders as they began to pour out of the ranch yard.

He hoisted her up into the roan's saddle, then climbed up behind her.

"You'll have to point out the way," he muttered. "I hope the roan can last."

Up on the east side of South Pass, where the land fell in a steep sliding pitch toward the Rio Grande and the mountain-locked country known as the Triangle, a small, cat-footed man kept his vigil. Apache Joe had a hermit's nature; he liked his own company best. He had a lean-to on Table Rock, overlooking the gap through Broken Crown, which protected him from the elements, and food was brought to him every two or three weeks.

This was the south entrance to Crown Basin, to Buck Stringer's desolate empire, and Apache Joe guarded its portal with loyal vigilance. A stranger coming through would be marked by a puff of smoke, Indian fashion, from Table Rock. A party of men rated three quick puffs, repeated at timed intervals.

From Table Rock the smoke signals could be seen at Broken Crown, and it was the method by which Buck Stringer could be apprised of intruders into his kingdom.

Apache Joe was coming down the sloping side of Broken Crown when he spotted the rider far below. Behind this double-burdened horse a dust cloud marked many horsemen. He squatted on his heels and studied the scene through sharp, beady eyes.

Trouble seldom came from within the Basin, but he sensed trouble now. Rising, he made his way to Flat Rock and darted inside his lean-to. He had a pair of Army field glasses there. He brought them out and put his attention on the nearer horseman. The glasses brought Luke Riatt and Rosalie into clear focus—he recognized Buck Stringer's girl immediately, and surprise flickered briefly across his weather-roughened face.

Swiveling slightly, he picked up the distant pursuers. He could not make out appearances, but he knew that the riders were Broken Crown men.

He squatted again, patiently, until he was sure that the double-burdened horse was headed for South Pass. Then he picked up his carbine and made his way to a jut of rock overlooking the Pass's approach. He squatted on his heels and made himself a limp cigaret which he stuck in a corner of his mouth. He did not light it. He waited until the rider was in clear and easy range below; then he brought the carbine up to his shoulder and squinted down the glinting barrel. . . .

The afternoon had worn away behind Riatt. All at once the sun was a reddening ball on the far hills; its rays lost their brutal impact. The shadows came away from the near rises, invading the Basin with silent swiftness.

The roan began to tire. He had carried a double burden too long, and now Luke felt his powerful muscles begin to quiver. The Ranger looked back to the men behind and he felt the weight of time on him, like a giant's hand. He had to get through. He had little doubt that Captain Hughes and his Rangers were on their way to the grim rendezvous with death in Placerita Canyon!

He felt the girl stir against him and look toward the barrier looming up ahead. "To the left," she murmured. "South Pass lies there—" And then she looked up into his face, fear stirring in her dark eyes. "Apache Joe, Luke! I almost forgot! He guards South Pass!"

Luke stiffened. He should have guessed, from Vince Stringer's warning. Buck Stringer and twenty hardcase riders rode behind, slowly closing in; up ahead a rifle barred his way. The big Ranger's eyes were bleak and foreboding as he weighed his chances.

The cut of South Pass loomed up ahead, dark and still—but the sun was still bright on the steep rough slope of Broken Crown. Luke's glance searched the broken pitch under the barrier's rim. He saw nothing, and for a brief moment he held the hope that Apache Joe was not at his post.

Then the carbine on the east wall opened up and lead splatted off the rock so close that the roan shied violently and nearly unseated them.

Luke jerked the animal toward the temporary protection of off-trail boulders as another slug screamed just behind them. He slid out of the saddle, jerking his Winchester free of its saddle boot.

The girl clung to the roan, looking down at Luke with a trapped, frightened gaze. Luke unbuckled his saddle bag and reached inside for a box of cartridges; he thrust it into his pocket and smiled reassuringly at the girl.

"I'll keep him busy," he said sharply. "Ride, Rosalie. Give the roan his head and let him run. He'll take you through. You'll meet Captain Hughes in the town of Ciba if you ride all night. You've got to get to him before he leaves in the morning. Tell him about the trap waiting for him in Placerita Canyon!"

Rosalie started to shake her head. Luke

slapped the roan on the rump, his voice sharply commanding. "Go!"

The roan leaped ahead. Luke whirled and sighted up the wall and fired at the puff of black smoke that preceded Apache Joe's rifle crack. He saw a small man slide away from the shelter of a rock and head quickly back along the steep slope.

The roan was still running with free stride. Luke saw Rosalie and his horse vanish into the blackness of South Pass, and he knew then that they were out of reach of the rifleman on Broken Crown.

He made a break for the steep rise of the rim, keeping boulders and brush between him and the rifleman above. He had little purpose now, other than to gain height from which he could temporarily stop Buck Stringer and his men from running Rosalie down.

Luke headed for higher ground. Twice the rifle above him splatted lead almost in his face, and each time he drove the man higher and farther away with close-probing slugs from the Winchester in his hands.

Eventually he reached a point on the slope from which he held a commanding view of the trail below. He settled back here, with his shoulders against a huge boulder, a thorny bush screening him from below.

Somewhere above and to the left of him, he

knew, Apache Joe was circling. Down on the trail, Buck Stringer and the rest of Broken Crown were drawing close.

Luke slid the muzzle of his rifle over the lip of a small rock and tried a long shot at the big, thick-shouldered man leading the pack. He squeezed trigger just as one of Buck's men spurred along-side his boss. The outlaw took Luke's lead and spilled out of the saddle.

Buck pulled abruptly off the trail, heading for the sheltering rocks. Luke sent two fast shots after him and then waited, a thin smile on his face. Below him the Broken Crown crew was breaking up, scattering for the protection off trail.

For the moment he had the Stringer bunch pinned down at the entrance to South Pass. But somewhere above him Apache Joe was looking for him. The Ranger knew it was time to move when a bullet brushed his shoulder and smeared a leaden blotch on the rock where his rifle muzzle had rested.

He slid away to the left, making a running break for an old erosion crack in the slope. When he was temporarily exposed, a half-dozen rifles opened up on him from below. He made the cut without getting hit, but sweat chilled the small of his broad back.

How much longer would he be able to keep up this grim game of hide and seek?

The sun was gone now. Stillness lay heavy on

the Broken Crown, as though twilight laid a quieting hand over the land. Riatt kept moving, hidden by the narrow cut.

He climbed upward, a faint hope rising in him. It would be dark in less than an hour. If he could find a way up to the rim of Broken Crown—

The erosion cut petered out against the crumbling rock face of the barrier. The remaining fifty feet to the rim were unscalable. Luke's face hardened with disappointment.

Then he saw the old game trail angling across the base of the rock. It looked recently traveled, and hope flared up in the big Ranger again. He cast a long look around him, searching for Apache Joe. He saw no movement. He had to chance it.

He came out to the narrow trail and crawled along it, heading at an angle along the slanting slope. . . .

From a point above and to the right of Luke, Apache Joe glimpsed the Ranger just as Riatt slid down into one of the innumerable cuts scouring the slope below the rise of the wall. A smile cracked the leathery cast of his features.

He rose and waved to the men hidden among the rocks far below.

From the shelter of a trail-flanking boulder Buck Stringer saw him wave. He scowled at Meeker, crouched next to him.

"What's Joe signalin' for?"

Meeker shaded his eyes. "Looks like he wants

us to come up." He studied the play of Joe's hand. "I think he's got that Ranger trapped!"

Buck spat into the sand. "We waited long enough," he growled. "Let's go get him!"

The path Luke followed was an old game trail which followed the angle of the steep slope. As he followed it hope built up in him that it would somehow lead through Broken Crown and tie in with the road through South Pass on the other side of the barrier.

At a bend in the trail, just before it entered a riven crack in the wall, he came upon a recently discarded cigaret butt. Suspicion crowded him now. If Apache Joe was ahead of him, the narrow cut could provide a half dozen opportunities for ambush. Yet he could not turn back. He could hear the Broken Crown men working up the slope—he was being driven into this cut despite himself.

Gripping his rifle more alertly, the Ranger eased into the rocky slit.

The crack extended clear through Broken Crown. He followed it to a rocky ledge over-looking the Rio Grande. And there he stopped. For the ledge ended abruptly, sixty feet above the brown, heaving turbulence below. Above and below him the rock wall was sheer.

He turned to face the narrow cut through which he had come. Now he knew why Apache Joe had not tried to cut him off. He was trapped there, with nowhere to go except back through the cut which even now was filling with Broken Crown men.

He waited, feeling the remoteness of this place where he was about to die. The river ran deep and sullen below him, hemmed in by the rocky cliffs —the shadows were deep in that narrow gorge. The Ranger discarded his rifle and drew his Colt —the thought that Rosalie Stringer might have gotten through gave him some small comfort.

The minutes passed, and the shadows deepened. Then he heard the scuff of boots on rocks and faced the cut, his six-gun cocked.

Buck Stringer's harsh voice suddenly made its demand from the darkness of the slit in the wall.

"Riatt! We know we got you cornered on that ledge! Throw down yore gun!"

The Ranger sneered grimly. "Come out and get me, Buck!"

An ugly silence followed. Then a shadowy figure broke out into the ledge, followed by another. . . . Luke's Colt cut them down. The first man spilled forward on his face; the second fell back and tripped the third man coming through.

There was a momentary swirl of confusion and ragged firing; then Buck's snarling curses faded into the sullen stillness.

Luke reloaded and waited, a big man with his back to Death. In the years he had worn the bright badge pinned to his torn shirt he had faced death many times—he had eyed it in odd corners of that big and sprawling Texas land. He had never expected to die in bed—

Rock dust sifted down from the rim above him, warning him a split-second before Apache Joe's bullet lanced down. Luke moved like a startled cat, his right hand cutting up, his Colt booming and bucking in his fist.

Apache Joe heaved up, still clutching his carbine. He staggered and tripped and came down off the rim. He fell eighty feet, and his body bounced off the ledge five feet from where the Ranger stood. He slid off and dropped, a limp and broken thing, into the sullen, heaving waters below.

Riatt peered over the edge. He caught a glimpse of Joe's body as it came to the surface, pushed by some turbulence below; then it was sucked down and vanished around a bend in the river.

Something he saw just below the ledge brought a bleak light to his eyes. It was a long shot, he thought—but it was the only chance he would have.

He jammed his Colt hard into his holster and flung a last look toward the gash in the wall. Then he stepped off the ledge and dropped eighty feet to the heaving torrent below. . . .

Several minutes later Buck Stringer broke out

onto the ledge. A half-dozen of his men crowded after him.

They found the ledge empty. Riatt's rifle lay where he had dropped it a few feet from the edge. But the big Ranger was gone.

Buck glanced down into the dark river. Daylight was fading fast—it would be dark in a few minutes.

He glanced up to the rim of Broken Crown. "Joe!" he called. "Did you get him?"

Joe didn't answer him. A nagging disappointment made Buck irritable. He was thinking of the Cordero brothers, waiting for two hundred rifles —and Luke Riatt!

Cordero would get the rifles. To the devil with Riatt. There were bigger stakes than the Ranger. Luke was dead—Matilde and Ramon would have to accept that. They couldn't back out of their deal now!

He turned away from the edge. "Let's go," he ordered harshly. "I reckon Joe got the Ranger from the rim just before Riatt tagged him. Looks like they went into the river together. . . ."

CHAPTER SIXTEEN

Rosalie Stringer rode through a dark, strange land slumped in the roan's saddle. Weariness racked her slender body. She let Riatt's horse pick his own way through the starlit, desolate country bordering the canyon of the Rio Grande. Her will seemed dissipated in terror and uncertainty, and only when she saw in the far distance the sputter of town lights did she rouse and show interest.

Several times the big roan turned and whinnied questioningly, and she knew that the animal missed the big man who had been left behind. She looked at the dark barrier through which she had come. All that had happened since her flight from Broken Crown seemed a bleak and ugly dream, and there was nothing ahead of her but the shadows and the night. She shuddered violently and clung to the long mane of the roan.

The town lights vanished as she rode down into the darkness—then the roan shied away and snorted heavily.

Two men rode out of the darkness, and one of them reached quickly for her reins. She saw them in the starlight—dark-faced, stocky men with bandoliers crossing their ragged shirt fronts.

Half an hour later they brought her into a small canyon where a fire flickered, hidden by the hemming hills. It was a big camp, although there was now only one fire. . . . She sensed, as they led the roan toward that blaze, that there were many men watching from the darkness.

Matilde Cordero watched his men bring her to him. He was sipping mescal from a small gourd, squatting on his heels. A stocky, powerful man with a heavy brush mustache, he wore two pistols in his wide brass-studded belt.

His brother Ramon, smaller, ferret-quick, but two years older, was on his left, nervously puffing on a thin, crooked cheroot. Jose Ferrito, their emissary to Buck Stringer, was standing up just behind them, frowning.

The two Mexican rebels halted on the edge of the fireglow, and one of them dismounted and pulled Rosalie from the saddle. Jose Ferrito whistled in surprise.

"It is Buck Stringer's girl, Matilde. . . ."

The Mexican rebel boss knitted unruly brows. He spoke to her, using a guttural Spanish she understood.

"Where is your father?"

Terror kept her mouth closed. Her knees were weak. The man who had hauled her out of her saddle spoke harshly. "She was alone. She seemed not to know where she was going."

Ramon looked at his brother. "A trap, perhaps,"

he muttered. "I have never trusted Buck Stringer."

Matilde sucked at his mescal. His beady eyes had a long, thoughtful glint. "Perhaps." He put the gourd aside and took the knife from his sheath and held the blade over the small flame. When it was hot enough he turned and walked to the girl.

"Perhaps you will tell us now," he suggested. His voice was as soft as a woman's, as emotionless as Death.

Rosalie shrank away from him. She nodded, her words coming in a broken pattern. She told him all that had happened since noon.

Matilde turned to Ramon. His teeth gleamed white in the firelight. "We will wait for the *Señor* Stringer," he said. "Perhaps he will not be able to fulfill all of his bargain, eh, Ramon?"

Ramon shrugged. A small smile played around his thin, cruel lips. "A bargain is a bargain, Matilde," he murmured, and turned to give orders, one by one, to the men clustered in the darkness beyond the fire.

Matilde waited by the fire, squatted on his heels. He had traded the mescal for a long, crooked cheroot like the one his brother smoked. His agate black eyes reflected the dancing flames. Around him, in the shadows, were many men. But Matilde squatted on his haunches, alone with his thoughts and his dreams . . . with the long hot days and the dusty marches yet to come.

Ramon stood alert and restless on the edge of the fire. Somewhere in the night a bird whistled, and he tensed and glanced toward his stocky, bushy-headed brother. Matilde looked at him and nodded and fell back to brooding.

Ramon Cordero sighed.

Ten minutes later the pounding of hoofs signaled Buck Stringer's approach. They came into Matilde Cordero's camp, sixteen mounted men with two wagons rumbling behind them.

Buck halted in the shadows. He glanced at Ramon, then over to Matilde, squatting on his heels by the fire. He saw Jose standing just beyond the Mexican rebel chief. Then he gave a quick start when he saw the small figure of his daughter near the sabre-scarred *segundo*. Relief lightened the gnawing irritation which had ridden with him . . . but his relief faded as he caught the stir of unseen men beyond the campfire.

He swung down from his saddle and strode toward Matilde, looking big and solid in the night. He strode past the Mexican leader, brushed past Jose and stood over his daughter.

"Glad you picked her up," he said harshly. "I was afraid she might have gotten past you." He put a hand on her shoulder, and Matilde said: "You can have her—later!"

Buck scowled. "I'll take care of her now. She needs a lesson—"

"Later!" Matilde's voice was impatient. Ramon came up to stand beside his brother . . . his eyes were on Buck, cold and demanding. He said: "The rifles, *Señor* Stringer?"

Buck jerked a thumb toward the wagons| behind him.

Matilde rose. He nodded to Jose, who had not moved. The scarred man headed for the wagons, walking through the saddle-weary, mounted Broken Crown riders.

Buck faced Matilde, sensing a controlled patience in the Mexican that put him on the alert: "I said the rifles are in the wagons, with the ammunition I promised you!"

Matilde shrugged. "Then you do not mind if Jose checks?"

Buck choked back his anger. He felt the unseen men in the shadows, watching, and knew the weight of the odds against him. It had not occurred to him that Cordero would try to take things into his own hands; he had never rated the stolid Mexican that high. He had considered him a small man with a rabble following . . . a minor nuisance along the Texas Border.

His uneasiness stirred a sudden anger in him. "Don't push me, Matilde!" he warned harshly. He stared grimly at Ramon. "I'm not one of yore scared Mexican *jefes*, ready to run when you ride into his town!"

Ramon said nothing; his smile was thin as the

edge of a cutting blade. Matilde made a gesture with his hands. He looked small beside Buck; he looked like some comic character, with his mustache and cartridge belts crossing his soiled white shirt.

"You promised me the Ranger Riatt," he said mildly. "I do not see him. How can I be sure about the rifles?"

Buck's jaw tightened grimly. "The rifles are in the wagon. I'm sorry about Luke Riatt. We had to kill him!"

Matilde's eyes glittered. "That was to be my pleasure—"

"To blazes with yore pleasure!" Buck growled. "This is no kid's game we're playin'! Tomorrow mornin' Captain Hughes and his Rangers will ride into Placerita Canyon. An' the day after that all of Triangle will be ours—"

"Yours!" Matilde said mildly. He smiled at Buck's stiffened features. "I am not the fool you thought, Buck. The massacre of Captain Hughes and his Rangers will be blamed on that Mexican outlaw from across the Border. Is that not so?"

Buck licked his lips. He had not planned it this way. But he knew what was going on in Matilde's head—and a helpless anger quivered in him. He had underrated this man all along.

He started to back away. "Yo're a darn fool!" he blustered. "But if that's the way you feel—"

Matilde Cordero took the cheroot from his lips and smiled. That was the last thing Buck remembered—that white-toothed smile. From the shadows behind Matilde a carbine slammed. The bullet struck Buck in the chest, driving him back. He got his Colt cleared of his holster before he fell, riddled.

Broken Crown's mounted men, caught in a crossfire, milled and cursed and fired wildly. The flurry lasted less than five minutes. Then a shocked silence settled over the dark Mexican camp. . . .

CHAPTER SEVENTEEN

Stars lighted the blackness of the river gorge. Against the damp cliff wall rising from the swirling current a man moved. Chilled, dripping, Luke Riatt searched for hand and toe holds in the face of that cliff, a stubborn and implacable urgency driving him.

It took him more than an hour to reach the ledge from which he had jumped. His arm and shoulder muscles ached with the strain—his fingers were raw and bleeding.

He hauled himself onto the ledge and lay there, his muscles quivering with fatigue. He listened to the night and the stillness, broken only by the deep rush of water below him, and knew that Buck Stringer and his men were long gone.

It was a long chance he had taken. He had seen that the current swirled in an eddy below the ledge, and he had chanced that no hidden rocks lay just below that dark surface. There was enough of an overhang to hide him from casual survey from the ledge, if he survived the plunge and came in close to the cliff. He had guessed right so far.

He was still alive. But he was afoot and bone-weary—and somewhere beyond Broken Crown Buck Stringer would be joining up with the Cordero brothers. And he knew, without question, that Captain Hughes would be riding through Placerita Canyon in the morning.

Rosalie might have gotten through—but he couldn't be sure. And too much hinged on getting a warning through to Captain Hughes before he reached the canyon.

He shivered as a chill struck through his wet clothes. He had to keep moving. He found his rifle where he had dropped it. His Colt was still in his holster. He picked up the rifle and stepped over the bodies of the two men he had killed. Buck Stringer had not bothered with them, which indicated that the boss of Broken Crown had been in a hurry.

It was harder coming down off the high rocky rim in the darkness than it had been going up. Impatience tugged at him, and a growing feeling of disaster. He reached the road and turned to the Pass, and then he heard the horse snort in the darkness off trail.

He whirled, his rifle swinging around to the sound.

Something moved among the boulders flanking the trail. Had Buck left one of his riders behind to make sure of him?

The Ranger moved carefully, stalking the bulking shadow of the horse. He rounded a rock and came up on his toes, his eyes probing the gloom.

A gray horse stood over a sprawled figure, reins trailing. Luke remembered the man who had gotten in the way of the bullet he had intended for Buck. This could be the man. The gray turned and looked at Luke and shook his head. Bit irons jingled in the darkness.

"Came back to him, eh?" Luke muttered. "He must have treated you pretty well—"

The gray reached down and muzzled the dead man. Luke walked out into the open. His voice was soft, soothing. The gray watched him, rigid now. But he didn't break and run.

Luke reached him and took hold of the trailing reins. He patted the animal's flank. "One-man horse," he said gently. Looking down, he saw that the dead man was Slim Meeker.

The gray tossed its head as Luke mounted. It seemed reluctant to leave the body. Luke stroked the animal's neck, thinking of his roan and the girl who rode him. He said softly: "Let's go now, fella. There's nothing you can do for him here."

In the early morning hours, just before dawn, he ran across the Mexican camp. The gray had stopped to blow and suddenly gone rigid, ears pricking the night. A horse had snorted softly and moved into sight; a saddled, riderless horse!

Luke rode close, his rifle held ready. He came up and saw the Broken Crown brand on the animal, and a frown appeared between his eyes. He turned and rode slowly down into the canyon and came upon the sprawled bodies, men and horses, in the darkness.

The fire had died down to cold embers . . . Matilde and Ramon and their rag-tail band were gone. There was only a deep silence and the grim evidence of what had happened there.

Riatt hunkered down beside Buck's body. "Rode into a trap you didn't plan on," he muttered, and wasted little time wondering why the Corderos had broken with Stringer. Perhaps Matilde and Ramon had wanted it that way all along.

He remounted and turned the gray toward the southeast. If the horse held out he might make Placerita Canyon before Captain Hughes and Company D rode into the waiting guns of that rebel Mexican band. . . .

The boulder-strewn sides of Placerita Canyon were not so steep a man couldn't climb them. The road from Ciba ran through it. This was the way Captain Hughes and his Rangers would come—up from Ciba and across the flat plain and into the Canyon, on his way to the rendezvous south of Placerita where Luke Riatt presumably would be waiting.

Since dawn the Cordero brothers had been busy setting their trap. Fifty men were hidden among the rocks on the slopes at the entrance to the canyon—the main body was with him at the far end of the canyon road. Fifty men to bottle the remnants of Captain Hughes' force when it recoiled from the ambush at the end of the canyon.

The wagons were in the shade of the cottonwoods around the small spring. Rosalie Stringer was tied to the wheel of one of the wagons. He wanted her out of the way until the fighting was over—Matilde had other plans for Buck Stringer's comely daughter.

Now his men were at their posts, behind rock and brush. Jose was on the left flank, smoking, a quick, nervous man. . . . Ramon, quiet and deadly, was closer to the wagons. Matilde chewed on his unlighted cheroot. He stood in plain sight, fifty feet from the wagons, and watched the far eastern rim of the canyon.

He had sent a man up on that rim to watch for the approach of Ranger Company D. Now he saw that ragged figure appear, lined against the morning sky, and hold his rifle aloft, making a swoop with it toward Ciba.

Matilde's black eyes glittered. In the next hours he would pay for all the ill-fated skirmishes he had had with that Texas Border company of hard-eyed men.

One hundred yards behind Matilde, from the screen of a chokeberry bush, Luke Riatt watched the ragged figure on the rim, and knew he had arrived too late to warn Captain Hughes.

Beyond the small spring a rope corral held Cordero's horses. Luke saw his roan among them. The big stallion towered over most of the scrubby broncs of Matilde's rebel band.

Luke's rifle leveled on Matilde's back and his jaw ridged. Then he sighed. He couldn't shoot a man in the back, not even to warn Captain Hughes. . . .

There was no cover between him and the wagons, and he made no effort to hide. He stood up and started walking toward the girl, his hands held loose at his sides.

For half the distance to the wagons no one noticed him. All eyes were turned in the direction away from him. Then Matilde turned. He was starting for the wagons, his rifle held loosely across his body. He took three easy strides before the tall figure impinged on his vision.

He froze, a strangely comical figure in tattered white shirt and shaggy hair. Buck Stringer had told him Luke Riatt was dead—and he had believed him! In that instant of inactivity his mind screamed a curse at Buck Stringer—then he opened his mouth in a wild yell and took a quick, aimless shot at the Ranger.

Luke's Colt made a heavy, overriding smash of sound. Matilde tripped and fell and rolled over once and then lay still, a small, crumpled figure, his dreams of empire snuffed out.

Ramon had turned at Matilde's wild cry. For a dragging interval he couldn't believe what he saw. The wide-shouldered Ranger was running toward the wagons . . . and toward him, gun in hand! Behind Riatt he could see his brother on the ground, a small, unmoving figure.

Surprise held him, as it held the other on the slopes of the Placerita. When he finally moved to fire at Luke he was already going down, two of Riatt's bullets tearing deep into him.

Luke reached Rosalie's side and started to slash her feet. Off to the side Jose Ferrito broke from cover on the slope and ran toward Riatt. He fired his carbine from the hip, saw his shot go wild, and slid to a stop, steadying himself.

Luke's voice was harsh in the girl's ear. "Make a run for it! Past the spring—"

Ferrito's second slug nipped his side and splintered through the wagon. The Ranger spun around, cut down at the scarred man and saw Jose jerk to the impact of his lead.

Then from the top of the Canyon, from both rims, a volley of rifle fire blasted down, searching and finding the Mexican outlaws hidden on the slopes. A wild, terrified confusion broke that leaderless band. They lunged up out of cover and spilled down to the canyon floor, heading for the corralled horses.

Riatt caught hold of Rosalie's arm and pulled her back under the wagon. From the canyon rim tall, sharpshooting men came sliding, pouring fire in Cordero's fleeing men.

Riatt recognized Captain Hughes among them. It didn't make sense. Captain Hughes and Company should be riding up canyon, the way Buck Stringer had planned it.

With the Cordero brothers dead there was no leadership left in the Mexican rebel raiders' ranks. They broke and scattered, what was left of them.

Riatt watched as Captain Hughes regrouped his men. From the far end of the canyon came the sounds of ragged rifle fire.

"Luke!" Captain Hughes' voice was anxious. "Luke—you all right?"

Riatt nodded. He waited with Rosalie by the wagons, a tired, puzzled man with the badge still clinging by a shred of cloth to his shirt. He waited for Captain Hughes to come striding up to them.

Later, by the campfire, Riatt listened to Captain Hughes' explanation. Hughes was surprised that Luke had not understood why he and the company had been waiting up on the rim of the Placerita for Cordero and his men.

"You wrote me that Buck Stringer and the Cordero brothers were teaming up; that you knew for sure that they would be camped at this end of the Placerita this morning, and for me to come with all the men I could spare. You said this was our chance to wipe out both Border gangs." Captain Hughes fumbled inside his pocket and brought out a dog-eared envelope. "Here, read it yourself."

Luke read the letter Lee Stringer had put into Ranger code. Sawbones Smith had copied his handwriting well. Reading the letter, Riatt thought of Lee Stringer lying dead in the sun. He had believed in Lee's essential honesty, and the renegade Ranger had not let him down.

"You'll have to thank Lee Stringer for this," he said. He saw a puzzled look crease Captain Hughes' rugged face, and he knew he had a lot of explaining to do. But he was bone-tired, and there was something else that needed attending to . . . something he should settle now.

Captain Hughes saw Luke's eyes as they went to Rosalie Stringer huddled by the morning fire. Luke had told him what had happened back at the ranch and he felt sorry for the girl, the last of the wild Stringers!

He reached inside his coat pocket and took out his pipe and stuffed tobacco into the coated bowl. . . . He watched Luke walk to the girl, squat down beside her. . . . He saw the look on her face as she turned to Riatt, the smile that lighted her face.

Maybe, Captain Hughes thought as he lighted up, Rosalie Stringer wouldn't be alone after all. . . .

Center Point Large Print
600 Brooks Road / PO Box 1
Thorndike, ME 04986-0001 USA

(207) 568-3717

US & Canada:
1 800 929-9108
www.centerpointlargeprint.com